THORNS

Thorns

ROBERT SILVERBERG

NEW ENGLISH LIBRARY
TIMES MIRROR

For Jim and Judy Blish

First published in Great Brtiain by Rapp & Whiting in 1969
© 1967 by Robert Silverberg

*

FIRST NEL PAPERBACK EDITION MAY 1977

*

NEL Books are published by
New English Library Limited from Barnard's Inn, Holborn, London EC1N 2JR
Made and printed in Great Britain by Hunt Barnard Printing Ltd., Aylesbury, Bucks.

45003193 4

CAMILLA: You, sir, should unmask.

STRANGER: Indeed?

CASSILDA: Indeed it's time. We have all laid aside
           disguise but you.

STRANGER: I wear no mask.

CAMILLA: (Terrified, aside to Cassilda.) No mask?
           No mask?

The King in Yellow: Act 1 - Scene 2.

One

The Song the Neurons sang

'Pain is instructive,' Duncan Chalk wheezed.

On crystal rungs he ascended the east wall of his office. Far on high was the burnished desk, the inlaid communicator box from which he controlled his empire. It would have been nothing for Chalk to sail up the wall on the staff of a gravitron. Yet each morning he imposed this climb on himself.

A variety of hangers-on accompanied him. Leontes d'Amore, of the mobile chimpanzee lips; Bart Aoudad; Tom Nikolaides, notable for shoulders. And others. Yet Chalk, learning the lesson of pain once more, was the focus of the group.

Flesh rippled and billowed on him. Within that great bulk were the white underpinnings of bone, yearning for release. Six hundred pounds of meat comprised Duncan Chalk. The vast leathery heart pumped desperately, flooding the massive limbs with life. Chalk climbed. The route zigged and back-switched up forty feet of wall to the throne at the top. Along the way blotches of thermoluminescent fungus glowed eagerly, yellow asters tipped with red, sending forth pulsations of warmth and brightness.

Outside it was winter. Thin strands of new snow coiled in the streets. The leaden sky was just begining to respond to the morning ionization poured into it by the great pylons of day. Chalk grunted. Chalk climbed.

Aoudad said, 'The idiot will be here in eleven minutes, sir. He'll perform.'

'Bores me now,' Chalk said. 'I'll see him anyway.'

'We could try torturing him,' suggested the sly d'Amore in a feathery voice. 'Perhaps then his gift of numbers would shine more brightly.'

Chalk spat. Leontes d'Amore shrank back as though a stream of acid had come at him. The climb continued. Pale fleshy hands reached out to grasp gleaming rods. Muscles

7

snarled and throbbed beneath the slabs of fat. Chalk flowed up the wall, barely pausing to rest.

The inner messages of pain dizzied and delighted him. Ordinarily he preferred to take his suffering the vicarious way, but this was morning, and the wall was his challenge. Up. Up. Toward the seat of power. He climbed, rung by rung by rung, heart protesting, intestines shifting position inside the sheath of meat, loins quivering, the very bones of him, flexing and sagging with their burden.

About him the bright-eyed jackals waited. What if he fell? It would take ten of them to lift him to the walkway again. What if the spasming heart ran away in wild fibrillation? What if his eyes glazed as they watched?

Would they rejoice as his power bled away into the air?

Would they know glee as his grip slipped and his iron grasp over their lives weakened?

Of course. Of course. Chalk's thin lips curved in a cool smile. He had the lips of a slender man, the lips of a bedouin burned down to bone by the sun. Why were his lips not thick and liquid?

The sixteenth rung loomed. Chalk seized it. Sweat boiled from his pores. He hovered a moment, painstakingly shifting his weight from the ball of the left foot to the heel of the right. There was no reward and less delight in being a foot of Duncan Chalk. For an instant nearly incalculable stresses were exerted across Chalk's right ankle. Then he eased forward, bringing his hand down across the last rung in a savage chopping motion, and his throne opened gladly to him.

Chalk sank into the waiting seat and felt it minister to him. In the depths of the fabric the micropile hands stirred and squeezed, soothing him. Ghostly ropes of spongy wire slid into his clothes to sponge the perspiration from the valleys and mounds of his flesh. Hidden needles glided through epithelium, squirting beneficial fluids. The thunder of the over-taxed heart subsided to a steady murmur. Muscles that had been bunched and knotted with exertion went slack. Chalk smiled. The day had begun; all was well.

Leontes d'Amore said, 'It amazes me, sir, how easily you make that climb.'

'You think I'm too fat to move?'

'Sir, I –'

'The fascination of what's difficult,' said Chalk. 'It spins the world on its bearings.'

'I'll bring the idiot,' d'Amore said.

'The idiot-savant,' Chalk corrected him. 'I have no interest in idiots.'

'Of course. The idiot-savant. Of course.'

D'Amore slipped away through an irising slot in the rear wall. Chalk leaned back, folding his arms over the seamless expanse of chest and belly. He looked out across the great gulf of the room. It was high and deep, an open space of large extent through which glowworms floated. Chalk had an old fondness for luminous organisms. Let there be light, be light, be light; if he had had the time, he might have arranged to glow himself.

Far below on the floor of the room, where Chalk had been at the commencement of the daily climb, figures moved in busy patterns, doing Chalk's work. Beyond the walls of the room were other offices, honeycombing the octagonal building whose core this was. Chalk had built a superb organization. In a large and indifferent universe he had carved out a sizable private pocket, for the world still took its pleasure in pain. If the deliciously morbid thrills of mulling over details of mass murders, war casualties, air accidents, and the like were largely things of the past, Chalk was well able to provide stronger, more extreme, and more direct substitutes. He worked hard, even now, to bring pleasure to many, pain to a few, pleasure and pain at once to himself.

He was uniquely designed by the accident of genes for his task: a pain-responsive, pain-fed eater of emotion, depending on his intake of raw anguish as others did on their intake of bread and meat. He was the ultimate representative of his audience's tastes and so was perfectly able to supply that vast audience's inner needs. But though his capacity had dwindled with the years, he still was not satiated. Now he picked his way through the emotional feasts he staged, a fresh gobbet here, a bloody pudding of senses there, saving his own appetite for the more grotesque permutations of cruelty, searching always for the new, and terribly old, sensations.

Turning to Aoudad, he said, 'I don't think the idiot-savant will be worth much. Are you still watching over the starman Burris?'

'Daily, sir.' Aoudad was a crisp man with dead gray eyes and a trustworthy look. His ears were nearly pointed. 'I keep watch over Burris.'

'And you, Nick? The girl?'

'She's dull,' said Nikolaides. 'But I watch her.'

'Burris and the girl . . . ' Chalk mused. 'The sum of two grudges. We need a new project. Perhaps . . . perhaps . . . '

D'Amore reappeared, sliding from the opposite wall atop a jutting shelf. The idiot-savant stood placidly beside him. Chalk leaned forward, doubling fold of belly over fold of belly. He feigned interest.

'This is David Melangio,' d'Amore said.

Melangio was forty years old, but his high forehead was unfurrowed and his eyes were as trusting as a child's. He looked pale and moist, like something out of the earth. D'Amore had dressed him stylishly in a glittering robe shot through with iron threads, but the effect was grotesque on him; the grace and dignity of the expensive garment were lost, and it served only to highlight Melangio's blank boyish innocence.

Innocence was not a commodity the public would pay any great price to buy. That was Chalk's business: supplying the public with what it demanded. Yet innocence coupled with something else might fill the current need.

Chalk played with the computer node at his left hand and said, 'Good morning, David. How do you feel today?'

'It snowed last night. I like the snow.'

'The snow will be gone soon. Machines are melting it.'

'I wish I could play in the snow.' Wistfully.

'You'd chill your bones,' said Chalk. 'David, what day was February 15, 2002?'

'Friday.'

'April 20, 1968?'

'Saturday.'

'How do you know?'

'It has to be like that,' said Melangio simply.

'The thirteenth President of the United States?'

'Fillmore.'

'What does the President do?'

'He lives in the White House.'

'Yes, I know,' said Chalk mildly, 'but what are his duties?'

'To live in the White House. Sometimes they let him out.'

'What day of the week was November 20, 1891?'

'Friday.' Instantly.

'In the year 1811, in which months did the fifth day fall on a Monday?'

'Only August.'

'When will February 29 next fall on a Saturday?'

10

Melangio giggled. 'That's too easy. We only get a February 29 once every four years, so – '

'All right. Explain Leap Year to me,' said Chalk.

Blankness.

'Don't you know why it happens, David?'

D'Amore said, 'He can give you any date over nine thousand years, sir, starting from the year 1. But he can't explain anything. Try him on weather reports.'

Chalk's thin lips quirked. 'Tell me about August 14, 2031, David.'

The high, piping voice responded: 'Cool temperatures in the morning, rising to a hundred and three along the eastern seaboard by two in the afternoon when the overload coils cut in. At seven p.m. the temperature was down to eighty-two, where it remained past midnight. Then it started to rain.'

'Where were you that day?' Chalk asked.

'At home with my brother and my sister and my mother and my father.'

'Were you happy that day?'

'?'

'Did anyone hurt you that day?' Chalk said.

Melangio nodded. 'My brother kicked me here, in my shin. My sister pulled my hair. My mother made me eat chemifix for breakfast. Afterward I went out to play. A boy threw a rock at my dog. Then – ?'

The voice was free of emotion. Melangio repeated his boyhood agonies as blandly as though he were giving the date of the third Tuesday in September, 1794. Yet beneath the glassy surface of prolonged childishness lay real pain. Chalk sensed it. He let Melangio drone on, occasionally prompting him with a guiding question.

Chalk's eyelids slipped together. It was easier to throw forth the receptors that way, to reach out and drain the substratum of sorrow that had its existence beneath David Melangio's trick brain. Old tiny griefs flowed like arcing currents across the room: a dead goldfish, a shouting father, a naked girl turning with heaving rosy-tipped breasts to utter words that killed. Everything was there, everything was accessible: the raw, maimed soul of David Melangio, forty years old, a human island well walled off from the stormy sea about him.

At length the recitation subsided. Chalk had had enough nourishment for now; he wearied of pushing Melangio's buttons. He tapered off by returning to the idiot-savant's strange powers of recall.

'David, catch these numbers: 96748759.'

'Yes.'

'And these: 32807887.'

'Yes.'

'Also: 333141187698.'

Melangio waited. Chalk said, 'Now, David.'

Numbers gushing in a smooth stream. '9674875932807887-333141187698.'

'David, how much is seven times twelve?'

A pause. 'Sixty-four?'

'No. Take nine from sixteen.'

'Ten?'

'If you can memorize the whole calendar upside down and backward, why can't you do arithmetic?'

Melangio smiled pleasantly. He said nothing.

'David, do you ever wonder why you are as you are?'

'As what?' Melangio asked.

Chalk was satisfied. The only pleasures to be extracted from David Melangio were low-level ones. Chalk had had his mild jolt of pleasure for the morning, and the faceless public would find a flicker of amusement in Melangio's freakish abilities to reel off dates, numbers, weather reports. But no one would draw real nourishment from David Melangio.

'Thank you, David,' Chalk said in easy dismissal.

D'Amore looked ruffled. His prodigy had failed to awe the big man, and d'Amore's continued prosperity depended on making frequent impacts here. Those who did not generally did not long remain in Chalk's service. The shelf in the wall retracted, taking d'Amore and Melangio away.

Chalk contemplated the gleaming rings imprisoned in ridges of fat on his short, thick fingers. He sat back then, closing his eyes. The image came to him of his body made up of concentric inner cores, like an onion, only with each discrete layer insulated from its neighbors by a sheet of quicksilver. The separate strata of Duncan Chalk slipping and sliding across one another, well lubricated, moving slowly as the quicksilver yielded to pressures and squirted down dark channels . . .

To Bart Aoudad he said, 'We must investigate the starman a little further.'

Aoudad nodded. 'I'll monitor the tracers, sir.'

To Tom Nikolaides Chalk said, 'And the girl. The dreary

little girl. We'll try an experiment. Synergy. Catalysis. Bring them together. Who knows? We might generate some pain. Some human feeling. Nick, we can learn lessons from pain. It teaches us that we're alive.'

'This Melangio,' Aoudad pointed out. 'He doesn't seem to feel his pain. He registers it, he engraves it on his brain. But he doesn't feel it.'

'Exactly,' said Chalk. 'My entire point. He can't feel anything, only record and replay. The pain's there, enough of it. But he can't reach it.'

'What if we liberated it for him?' suggested Aoudad. He smiled, not pleasantly.

'Too late. He'd burn up in an instant if he could ever really reach that pain now. No, leave him to his calendars, Bart. Let's not destroy him. He'll do his trick, and everyone will applaud, and then we'll drop him back into his puddle. The starman, though – that's something else again.'

'And the girl,' Nikolaides reminded him.

'Yes. The starman and the girl. It should be interesting. We should learn a great deal.'

Two

On Earth as in Heaven

Long afterward, when fresh blood would stain his hands and his heart would pound with the surge of renewed life, it might all begin to seem like no more than an ugly, nasty dream to him. But he'd have to cross Heimdall's shining bridge to get there. Just now he still lived in pain, and he felt now as he had felt while it was happening. Many terrors enfolded Minner Burris.

He was not a man normally vulnerable to terror. But this had been too much: the great greasy shapes moving about his ship, the golden manacles, the case of surgical instruments open and ready.

'——,' the pockmarked monster to his left had said.

'— —— ——,' the creature on the other side had replied in what sounded like unctuous terms.

13

Then they had begun the work of destroying Minner Burris.

Then was then and now was now, but Burris carried about a load of pain and strangeness that eternally reminded him, waking or sleeping, of the thing that had been done to him behind the cloak of darkness, beyond the unspinning chill of Pluto.

He had returned to Earth three weeks ago. He lived now in a single room of the Martlet Towers, supported by a government pension and propped somehow by his own inner resilience. To be transformed by monsters into a monster was no easy fate to accept, but Burris was doing his best.

If only there were not so much pain –

The doctors who had examined him had been confident at first that they could do something about the pain. All it took was the application of modern medical technology.

' – damp down the sensory intake – '

' – minimal dosage of drugs to block the afferent channels, and then – '

' – minor corrective surgery – '

But the lines of communication within Burris's body were hopelessly scrambled. Whatever the alien surgeons had done to him, they had certainly transformed him into something that was beyond the comprehension, let alone the capabilities, of modern medical technology. Ordinary pain-killing drugs merely intensified Burris's sensations. His patterns of neutral flow were bizarre; sensation was shunted, baffled, deflected. They could not repair the damage the aliens had done. And finally Burris crept away from them, throbbing, mutilated, aggrieved, to hide himself in a dark room of this moldering residential colossus.

Seventy years before, the Martlet Towers had been the last word in dwelling-places: sleek mile-high edifices arrayed in serried ranks along the formerly green slopes of the Adriondacks, within easy commuting distance of New York. Seventy years is a long time in the lifetime of contemporary buildings. Now the Towers were corroded, pitted by time, transfixed by the arrows of decay. Suites of earlier resplendence were subdivided into single-room warrens. An ideal place to hide, Burris thought. One nestled into one's cell here like a polyp within its limestone cave. One rested; one thought; one worked at the strenuous task of coming to terms with what had been committed upon one's helpless form.

Burris heard scrabbling sounds in the corridors. He did not

investigate. Whelks and prawns, mysteriously mutated for land life, infiltrating the crawl spaces of the building? Millipedes seeking the sweet warmth of leaf mold? Toys of the dull-eyed children? Burris stayed in the room. He often thought of going out at night, prowling the passages of the building like his own ghost, striding through darkness to strike terror into chance beholders. But he had not left the four walls since the day he had rented – by proxy – this zone of calm in tempest.

He lay in bed. Pale green light filtered through the walls. The mirror could not be removed, for it was part of the structure of the building, but it could at least be neutralized; Burris had switched it off, and it was nothing now but a dull brown oblong on the wall. From time to time he activated it and confronted himself, as discipline. Perhaps, he thought, he would do that today.

When I rise from bed.

If I rise from bed.

Why should I rise from bed?

There was an inner spike embedded in his brain, clamps gripping his viscera, invisible nails riveting his ankles. His eyelids sandpapered his eyes. Pain was a constant, even growing now to become an old friend.

What was it the poet said? The *withness* of the body . . .

Burris opened his eyes. They no longer opened up and down, as human eyes did. Now the membranes that served as lids slid outward from the center toward the corners. Why? Why had the alien surgeons done any of it? But this in particular seemed to serve no valid purpose. Top-and-bottom eyelids were good enough. These did not improve the function of the eyes; they served only to act as intrusive wardens against any sort of meaningful communication between Burris and the human race. At each blink he shouted his weirdness.

The eyes moved. A human eye moves in a series of tiny jerking motions, which the mind melds together into an abstraction of unity. Burris's eyes moved as the panning eye of a camera would move if cameras were perfectly mounted: smoothly, continuously, unflickeringly. What Burris saw lacked glamour. Walls, low ceiling, neutralized mirror, vibrator sink, food conduit hatch, all the drab appurtenances of a simple low-cost room designed for self-sufficiency. The window had been kept opaqued since he had moved in. He had no idea of time of day, of weather, even of season, though it had been

15

winter when he came here and he suspected that it was winter still. The lighting in the room was poor. Squibs of indirect illumination emerged on a random pattern. This was Burris's period of low receptivity to light. For days at a time the world at its brightest seemed a murky darkness to him, as though he were at the bottom of a muddy pond. Then the cycle would reverse itself with an unpredictable flip, and a few photons would be sufficient to light up his brain in a wild blaze.

Out of the murk came the image of his vanished self. The obliterated Minner Burris stood in a blunted corner of the room, studying him.

Dialogue of self and soul.

'You're back, you filthy hallucination!'

'I won't ever leave you.'

'All I have, is that it? Well, make yourself welcome. A bit of cognac? Accept my humble hospitality. Sit down, sit down!'

'I'll stand. How are you coming along, Minner?'

'Poorly. A lot you care.'

'Is that a note of self-pity I detect in your voice?'

'What if it is? What if it is?'

'A terrible voice, and one that I never taught you.'

Burris could not sweat any longer, but a cloud of vapor gathered over each of his new exhalator pores. He stared fixedly at his former self. In a low voice he said, 'Do you know what I wish? That they'd get hold of you and do to you what they did to me. Then you'd understand.'

'Minner, Minner, it's already been done to me! *Ecce homo!* There you lie to prove that I've been through it!'

'No. There you stand to prove that you haven't. Your face. Your pancreas. Your liver and lights. Your skin. It hurts, it hurts – it hurts me, not you!'

The apparition smiled gently. 'When did you begin feeling so sorry for yourself? This is a new development, Minner.'

Burris scowled. 'Perhaps you're right.' The eyes smoothly scanned the room from wall to wall again. He muttered, 'They're watching me, that's the trouble.'

'Who is?'

'How would I know? Eyes. Telelenses in the walls. I've searched for them, but it's no use. Two molecules in diameter – how am I ever going to find them? And they see me.'

'Let them look, then. You have nothing to be ashamed of. You're neither pretty nor ugly. There's no point of reference for you. I think it's time you went outside again.'

'It's easy for you to say that,' Burris snapped. 'No one stares at *you*.'

'You're staring at me right now.'

'So I am,' Burris admitted. 'But you know why.'

With a conscious effort he induced the phase-shift to begin. His eyes dealt with the light in the room. He no longer had retinas, but the focus-plates embedded against his brain served well enough. He looked at his former self.

A tall man, broad-shouldered and blocky, with heavy muscles and thick sandy hair. So he had been. So he was now. The alien surgeons had left the underlying structure intact. But all else was different.

The vision of self before him had a face nearly as wide as it was high, with generous cheekbones, small ears, and dark eyes set far apart. The lips were the sort that compress themselves easily into a rather fussy line. A light powdering of freckles covered the skin; there was fine golden hair almost everywhere on him. The effect was routinely virile: a man of some strength, some intelligence, some skill, who would stand out in a group not by virtue of any conspicuous positive trait but by grace of a whole constellation of inconspicuous positive traits. Success with women, success with other men, success in his profession – all those things accompanied such triumphant unspectacular attractiveness.

All that was gone now.

Burris said quietly, 'I don't mean to sound self-pitying now. Kick me if I whine. But do you remember when we would see hunchbacks? A man with no nose? A girl folded into herself with no neck and half an arm? Freaks? Victims? And we'd wonder what it was like to be hideous.'

'You're not hideous, Minner. Just different.'

'Choke on your stinking semantics! I'm something that everyone would stare at now. I'm a monster. Suddenly I'm out of your world and into the world of the hunchbacks. They know damned well that they can't escape all those eyes. They cease to have independent existences and blur into the fact of their own deformities.'

'You're projecting, Minner. How can you know?'

'Because it's happening to me. My whole life now is built around what the Things did to me. I don't have any other existence. It's the central fact, the only fact. How can we

2   17

know the dancer from the dance? I can't. If I ever went outside, I'd be on constant display.'

'A hunchback has a lifetime to get used to himself. He forgets his back. You're still new at this. Be patient, Minner. You'll come to terms. You'll forgive the staring eyes.'

'How soon? *How soon?*'

But the apparition was gone. Prodding himself through several shifts of vision, Burris searched the room and found himself again alone. He sat up, feeling the needles pricking his nerves. There was no motion without its cluster of discomforts. His body was ever with him.

He stood up, rising in a single fluid motion. This new body gives me pain, he told himself, but it is efficient. I must come to love it.

He braced himself in the middle of the floor.

Self-pity is fatal, Burris thought. I must not wallow. I must come to terms. I must adjust.

I must go out into the world.

I was a strong man, not just physically. Is all my strength – *that* strength – gone now?

Within him coiling tubes meshed and unmeshed. Tiny stopcocks released mysterious hormones. The chambers of his heart performed an intricate dance.

They're watching me, Burris thought. Let them watch! Let them get a good eyeful!

With a savage swipe of his hand he switched on the mirror and beheld his naked self.

Three

Subterranean Rumbles

Aoudad said, 'What if we traded? You monitor Burris, I'll watch the girl. Eh?'

'Nix.' Nikolaides drew the final consonant out luxuriously. 'Chalk gave her to me, him to you. She's a bore, anyway. Why switch?'

'I'm tired of him.'

'Put up with him,' Nikolaides advised. 'Unpleasantness is up-building to character.'

'You've been listening to Chalk too long.'

'Haven't we all?'

They smiled. There would be no trade of responsibilities. Aoudad jabbed at the switch, and the car in which they were riding cut sharply from one mastercom network to the other. It began rocketing northward at a hundred and fifty miles an hour.

Aoudad had designed the car himself, for Chalk's own use. It was a womb, more or less, lined with soft warm pink spongy fibers and equipped with every sort of comfort short of gravi-trons. Chalk had wearied of it lately and was willing to let underlings make use of it. Aoudad and Nikolaides rode it often. Each man considered himself Chalk's closest associate; each quietly considered the other a flunky. It was a useful mutual delusion.

The trick was to establish some sort of existence for yourself independent of Duncan Chalk. Chalk demanded most of your waking hours and was not above using you in your sleep when he could. Yet there was always some fragment of your life in which you stood apart from the fat man and regarded yourself, as a rounded, self-guiding human being. For Nikolaides the answer lay in physical exertion: skimming lakes, hiking to the rim of a boiling sulfurous volcano, sky-paddling, desert-drilling. Aoudad had chosen exertion, too, but of a softer kind; legs spread and toe touching toe, his women would form a trestle stretching across several continents. D'Amore and the others had their own individual escapes. Chalk devoured those who did not.

Snow was falling again. The delicate flakes perished almost as soon as they landed, but the car-track was slippery. Servo-mechanisms quickly adjusted the tracking equipment to keep the car upright. Its occupants reacted in different ways; Niko-laides quickened at the thought of the potential danger, minute though it was, while Aoudad thought gloomily of the eager thighs that awaited him if he survived the journey.

Nikolaides said, 'About this trade – '

'Forget it. If the answer's no, the answer's no.'

'I just want to find out. Tell me this, Bart: are you interested in the girl's body?'

Aoudad recoiled in excessive innocence. 'What the hell do you think I am?'

19

'I know what you are, and so does everyone else. But I'm just fishing around. Do you have some odd idea that if we switch assignments and you get Lona, you'll be able to have her?'

Sputtering, Aoudad said, 'I draw the line at some women. I'd never meddle with her. For Christ's sake, Nick! The girl is too dangerous. A seventeen-year-old virgin with a hundred kids – I wouldn't touch her! Did you really think I would?'

'Not really.'

'Why'd you ask, then?'

Nikolaides shrugged and stared at the snow.

Aoudad said, 'Chalk asked you to find out, is that it? He's afraid I'll molest her, is that it? Is it? Is it?' Nikolaides did not answer, and suddenly Aoudad began to tremble. If Chalk could suspect him of such desires, Chalk must have lost all faith in him. The compartments were separate: work here, women there. Aoudad had never straddled those compartments yet, and Chalk knew it. What was wrong? Where had he failed the fat man? Why had faith been withdrawn this way?

Aoudad said hollowly, 'Nick, I swear to you I had no such intentions in proposing a switch. The girl doesn't interest me sexually at all. Not at *all*. You think I want a goddam grotesque kid like that? All I had in mind was I was tired of looking at Burris's mixed-up body. I wanted variety in my assignment. And you – '

'Cut it out, Bart.'

' – read all sorts of sinister and perverse – '

'I didn't.'

'Chalk did, then. And you went along with him. Is this a plot? Who's out to get me?'

Nikolaides nudged his left thumb into the dispenser button, and a tray of relaxers popped out. Quietly he handed one to Aoudad, who took the slender ivory-colored tube and pressed it to his forearm. An instant later the tension ebbed. Aoudad tugged at the pointed tip of his left ear. That had been a bad one, that surge of tension and suspicion. They were coming more frequently now. He feared that something nasty was happening to him and that Duncan Chalk was tapping in on his emotions, drinking in the sensations as he passed on a pre-destined course through paranoia and schizophrenia to catatonic suspension.

I will not let it happen to me, Aoudad resolved. He can have his pleasures, but he won't get his fangs into *my* throat.

'We'll remain on our assignments until Chalk says otherwise, yes?' he said aloud.

'Yes,' Nikolaides replied.

'Shall we monitor them as we ride along?'

'No objections.'

The car was passing the Appalachia Tunnel now. High blank walls hemmed them in. The highway was steeply banked here, and as the car barreled along at a high-G acceleration, a gleam of sensual appreciation came into Nikolaides's eyes. He sat back in the huge seat meant for Chalk. Aoudad, beside him, opened the communication channels. The screens lit.

'Yours,' he said. 'Mine.'

He looked at his. Aoudad no longer shivered when he saw Minner Burris, but the sight was a spooky one even now. Burris stood before his mirror, thereby providing Aoudad with the sight of two of him.

'There but for the grace of something-or-other go we,' Aoudad murmured. 'How'd you like to have that done to you?'

'I'd kill myself instantly,' said Nikolaides. 'But somehow I think the girl's in a worse mess. Can you see her from where you're sitting?'

'What is she doing? She's naked?'

'Bathing,' said Nikolaides. 'A hundred children! Never been had by a man! The things we take for granted, Bart. Look.'

Aoudad looked. The squat bright screen showed him a nude girl standing under a vibraspray. He hoped that Chalk was fastened to his emotional stream right now, for as he looked at Lona Kelvin's bare body he felt nothing. Not a thing. No shred of sensuality.

She could not have weighed more than a hundred pounds. Her shoulders sloped, her face was wan, her eyes lacked sparkle. She had small breasts, a slender waist, narrow boyish hips. As Aoudad watched, she turned around, showing him flat, scarcely feminine buttocks, and switched off the vibraspray. She began to dress. Her motions were slow, her expression sullen.

'Maybe I'm prejudiced because I've been working with Burris,' Aoudad said, 'but it seems to me that he's very much more complicated than she is. She's just a dumb kid who's had a hard time. What will he see in her?'

'He'll see a human being,' said Nikolaides. 'That may be enough. Perhaps. Perhaps. It's worth a try, bringing them together.'

21

'You sound like a humanitarian,' Aoudad said in wonder.

'I don't like to see people hurting.'

'Who does, aside from Chalk? But how can you possibly get involved with these two? Where's the handle? They're too remote from us. They're grotesques. They're baroques. I don't see how Chalk can sell them to the public.'

Nikolaides said patiently, 'Individually they're baroques. Put them together and they're Romeo and Juliet. Chalk has a certain genius for things like that.'

Aoudad eyed the girl's empty face and then the eerie, distorted mask that was the face of Minner Burris. He shook his head. The car rocketed forward, a needle penetrating the black fabric of the night. He switched off the screens and shut his eyes. Women danced through his brain: real women, adults, with soft, rounded bodies.

The snow became thicker in the air about them. Even in the shielded snout of the womb-like car, Bart Aoudad felt a certain chill.

Four

Child of Storm

Lona Kelvin donned her clothes. Two undergarments, two overgarments, gray on gray, and she was dressed. She walked to the window of her little room and looked out. Snowfall. White swirls in the night. They could get rid of the snow fast enough once it hit ground, but they couldn't keep it from falling. Not yet.

A walk in the Arcade, Lona decided. Then sleep and another day put to rest.

She drew her jacket on. Shivered in anticipation. Looked about her.

Pasted neatly to the walls of the room were photographs of babies. Not a hundred babies; more like sixty or seventy. And not her babies. But sixty baby photographs might just as well be a hundred. And to a mother like Lona, any babies might be her babies.

They looked as babies look. Rounded, unshaped faces with button noses and glossy, drooling lips and unseeing eyes. Tiny ears, painfully perfect. Clutching little hands with improbably splendid fingernails. Soft skin. Lona reached out and touched the photograph nearest the door and imagined that she was touching baby-velvet. Then she put her hand to her own body. Touched the flat belly. Touched a small, hard breast. Touched the loins from which a legion of infants had and had not sprung. She shook her head in what might have been thought a self-pitying gesture, but most of the self-pity had been drained away by now, leaving only a gritty residual sediment of confusion and emptiness.

Lona went out. The door quietly sealed itself behind her.

The dropshaft took her swiftly to ground level. Wind whipped down the narrow passage between the tall buildings. Overhead, the artificial glow of night pressed back the darkness; colored globes moved silently to and fro. Snowflakes danced against them. The pavement was warm. The buildings that flanked her were brightly lit. To the Arcade, Lona's feet told her. To the Arcade to walk awhile in the brightness and the warmth of this snowy night.

Nobody recognized her.

Only a girl out by herself for the evening. Mouse-colored hair flipping about her ears. A thin-naped neck, slumping shoulders, an insufficient body. How old? Seventeen. Could be fourteen, though. No one asked. A mouse girl.

Mousy.

Dr Teh Ping Lin, San Francisco, 1966:

'At the scheduled time of hormonally induced ovulation, female mice of the black-agouti C3H/HeJ strain were caged with fertile males of an albino strain, either BALB/c or Cal A (originally A/Crgl/2). Nine to twelve hours after the expected mating, eggs were flushed from the oviducts, and fertilized eggs were identified by the presence of the second polar body or by observation of pronuclei.'

It was a taxing experiment for the doctor. Microinjection of living cells was nothing new even then, but work with mammalian cells had been flawed. The experimenters had not been able to safeguard the structural or functional integrity of the whole ovum.

No one had ever informed Lona Kelvin that:

'The mammalian egg is apparently more difficult to inject than other cells because of the thick zona pellucida and the vitelline membrane, both of which are highly elastic and resistant to the penetration of a microinstrument, especially at the unfertilized stage.'

Crowds of boys were gathered, as usual, in the vestibule that led to the Arcade. With some of them were girls. Lona eyed them shyly. Winter did not extend to this vestibule; the girls had shucked their thermal wraps and stood proudly on display. This one had given her nipples a phosphorescence. That one had shaved her skull to exhibit the fine bony structure. There, voluptuous in the final weeks of pregnancy, a redhead linked her arms with two tall young men and laughingly roared obscenities.

Lona viewed her, edge-on. Big belly, bulky burden. Can she see her toes? Her breasts are swollen. Do they hurt? The child was conceived in the old way. Lona blinked. Gasp and thrust and shudder in the loins and a baby made. *One* baby. Possibly two. Lona drew her narrow shoulders back, filled her pinched lungs with air. The gesture raised her breasts and thrust them outward, and color came to her angular cheeks.

'Going to the Arcade? Go with me.'

'Hey, robin! Let's chirp!'

'Need a friend, friend?'

Eddies of talk. Buzzing basso invitations. Not for her. Never for her.

I am a mother.

I am *the* mother.

'These fertilized eggs were then placed in a medium consisting of three parts modified Locke's solution, one part 2.9 percent sodium citrate dihydrate, and 25 mg of bovine gamma globulin (BGG, Armour) per milliliter of the citrate-Locke's solution. Penicillin (100 unit/ml) and streptomycin ($50\mu g/ml$) were added to the medium. Viscosity of the medium at $22°$ C was 1.1591 cp and its pH 7.2. Eggs were retained for micromanipulation and injection within a drop of the bovine gamma globuline-citrate-Locke's solution (GCL) which was covered with mineral oil in a vaseline well on a microscope slide.'

Tonight there was a small surprise for Lona. One of the loungers at the vestibule approached her. Was he drunk? So sexually deprived that she was attractive to him? Moved by pity for the waif? Or did he know who she was and wish to share her glory? That was the least probable of all. He did not know, would not wish. Of glory there was none.

He was no beauty, but not conspicuously repulsive. Of

24

medium height; black hair slicked straight forward almost to his eyebrows; eyebrows themselves slightly distorted surgically to arch in a skeptical inverted V; eyes gray, and bright with shallow craftiness; chin weak; nose sharp, prominent. About nineteen years old. Sallow skin marked with underlying striations, sun-sensitive patterns that would blaze in glory at noon. He looked hungry. On his breath a mixture of things: cheap wine, spiced bread, a hint of (splurge!) filtered rum.

'Hello, lovely. Let's match. I'm Tom Piper. Tom Piper's son. You?'

'Please – no,' Lona murmured. She tried to move away. He blocked her, exhaling.

'Matched already? Meeting someone inside?'

'No.'

'Why not me, then? You could do worse.'

'Let me be.' A faint whimper.

He leered. Small eyes boring into her own. 'Starman,' he said. 'Just in from the outer worlds. We'll get a table and I'll tell you all about them. Mustn't turn a starman down.'

Lona's forehead furrowed. Starman? Outer worlds? Saturn dancing within its rings, green suns beyond the night, pale creatures with many arms? He was no starman. Space marks the soul. Tom Piper's son was unmarked. Even Lona could tell that. Even Lona.

'You aren't,' she said.

'Am. I'll tell you the stars. Ophiuchus. Rigel. Aldebaran. I've been out there. Come on, flower. Come with Tom.'

He was lying. Glamorizing himself to enhance his magnetism. Lona shivered. Past his thick shoulder she saw the lights of the Arcade. He leaned close. His hand descended, found her hip, curled lasciviously over the flat haunch, the lean flank.

'Who knows?' he whispered huskily. 'The night could go anywhere. Maybe I'll give you a baby. I bet you'd like that. You ever had a baby?'

Her nails raked his cheek. He reeled back, surprised, bloodied, and for a moment the banded ornaments beneath his skin glowed brightly even in the artificial light. His eyes were wild. Lona swung around and sidestepped him, losing herself in the throng surging through the vestibule.

Elbows busy, she sliced a path into the Arcade.

Tom, Tom, the piper's son, give you a baby before he's done . . .

'Three hundred and one newly fertilized eggs were main-

25

tained in vaseline well preparations and each received one of the following experimental treatments: (i) no pipette puncture and no injection; (ii) puncture of egg but no injection; (iii) injection of $180\mu^3$ of the solution containing about 5 pg of BGG; (iv) injection of $770\mu^3$ of the solution containing 20 pg of BGG; or (v) injection of $2730\mu^3$ of the solution containing 68 pg of BGG.'

The Arcade glittered. Here were all the cheaper pleasures, gathered under one glassy roof. As Lona passed the gate, she thrust her thumb against the toller to register her presence and be billed for her visit. It was not costly to enter. But she had money, she had money. They had seen to that.

She planted her feet squarely and looked up at tier after tier, reaching toward the roof two hundred feet above. Up there snow was falling but not landing; efficient blowers kept it from touching the arching roof, and the flakes fell to a sticky death on the heated pavement.

She saw the gambling tiers where a man could play any game for any stake. The stakes were generally not high. This was a place for the young, for the purse-poor. For the grubby. But with a will a man could lose thickly here, and some had. Up there wheels turned, lights flashed, buttons clicked. Lona did not understand the gambling games.

Farther up, in mazy networks of corridors, flesh could be purchased by those with the need or the inclination. Women for men, men for women, boys for girls, girls for boys, and any conceivable combination. Why not? A human being was free to make disposition of his body in any way that did not directly interfere with the well-being of another. Those who sold were not forced to sell. They could become shopkeepers instead. Lona did not go to the houses of flesh.

Here on the main level of the Arcade were the booths of small merchants. A handful of coins would buy a pocketful of surprises. What about a tiny rope of living light to brighten the dull days? Or a pet from another world, so they said, though in truth the jewel-eyed toads were cultured in the laboratories of Brazil? What of a poetry box to sing you to sleep? Photographs of the great ones, cunningly designed to smile and speak? Lona wandered. Lona stared. Lona did not touch, did not buy.

'Viability of eggs was tested by transplantation into mated inbred albino BALB/c or Cal A recipients which were under anesthesia. The recipients had been induced by hormone

26

injection to ovulate simultaneously with the agouti C3H donors and had been mated with fertile males of their own albino strain.'

Someday my children will come here, Lona told herself. They'll buy toys. They'll enjoy themselves. They'll run through the crowds –

– a crowd all by themselves –

She sensed breath on her nape. A hand caressed her rump. Tom Piper? She turned in panic. No, no, not Tom Piper, just some giraffe of a boy who studiously stared upward at the distant tiers of the fleshmongers. Lona moved away.

'The entire procedure from the time experimental eggs were flushed from the donor oviduct to the time of their transplantation into the recipient infundibulum required 30 to 40 minutes. During this period of maintenance in vitro at room temperature many eggs shrank within their zonae pellucidae.'

Here was the zoo exhibit. Caged things pacing, peering, imploring. Lona went in. The last beasts, here? A world swept free of animals? Here was the giant anteater. Which was the snout, which the tail? A tree sloth lavishly hooked its claws into dead wood. Nervous coati-mundis paced their quarters. The stink of beasts was flogged from the room by whirring pumps beneath the flagstone floor.

' . . . the shrunken eggs usually survived and were regarded as essentially normal . . . '

The animals frightened Lona. She moved away, out of the zoo, circling the main gallery of the Arcade once again. She thought she saw Tom Piper pursuing her. She brushed lightly against the rigid belly of the pregnant girl.

' . . . the number of degenerating embryos and resorption sites was also examined in the autopsied recipients . . . '

She realized that she did not want to be here at all. Home, safe, warm, alone. She did not know which was more frightening: people in great herds, or one person, singly.

' . . . a fair number of eggs survive micromanipulation and injection of a foreign substance . . . '

I want to leave, Lona decided.

Exit. Exit. Where was the exit? Exits were not featured here. They wanted you to stay. Suppose fire broke out? Robots sliding from concealed panels, quenching the blaze. But I want to leave.

' . . . a useful method is thus provided . . . '

27

' . . . the survival of pronuclear eggs after the various treatments is shown in Table 1 . . . '

' . . . the fetuses which developed from the microinjected eggs were smaller more frequently than their native littermates, although no other external abnormality was observed . . . '

Thank you, Dr Teh Ping Lin of San Francisco.

Lona fled.

She rushed in a frenzied circle around the belly of the bright Arcade. Tom Piper found her again, shouted to her, reached forth his hands. He's friendly. He means no harm. He's lonely. Maybe he really is a starman.

Lona fled.

She discovered an exfundibulum and rushed to the street. The sounds of the Arcade dwindled. Out here in the darkness she felt calmer, and the sweat of panic dried on her skin, cooling her. Lona shivered. Looking over her shoulder many times, she hurried toward her building. Clasped to her thigh were anti-molestation weapons that would thwart any rapist: a siren, a screen of smoke, a laser to flash pulsations of blinding light. Yet one never could be certain. That Tom Piper; he could be anywhere and capable of anything.

She reached home. My babies, she thought. I want my babies.

The door closed. The light went on. Sixty or seventy soft images clung to the walls. Lona touched them. Did their diapers need changing? Diapers were an eternal verity. Had they gurgled milk over their rosy cheeks? Should she brush their curly hair? Tender skulls, not yet knit; flexible bones; snub noses. My babies. Lona's hands caressed the walls. She shed her clothes. A time came when sleep seized her.

Five

Enter Chalk; to him, Aoudad

Duncan Chalk had been studying the tapes on the pair for three days, giving the project nearly his undivided attention. It seemed to him now that he knew Minner Burris and Lona Kelvin as thoroughly as anyone had ever known them. It seemed to him, also, that the idea of bringing them together had merit.

Intuitively, Chalk had known that from the beginning. But, though he trusted his intuitive judgements, he rarely acted on them until he had had time to make a more rational reconnaissance. Now he had done that. Aoudad and Nikolaides, to whom he had delegated the preliminary phases of this enterprise, had submitted their selections of the monitor tapes. Chalk did not rely on their judgement alone; he had arranged for others to scan the tapes as well and prepare their own anthologies of revealing episodes. It was gratifying to see how well the choices coincided. It justified his faith in Aoudad and Nikolaides. They were good men.

Chalk rocked back and forth in his pneumatic chair and considered the situation while all about him the organization he had built hummed and throbbed with life.

A project. An enterprise. A joining of two suffering human beings. But were they human? They had been, once. The raw material had been human. A sperm, an ovum, a set of genetic codons. A whimpering child. So far, so good. A small boy, a small girl, blank planchets ready for life's imprint. Life had come down hard on these two.

Minner Burris. Starman. Intelligent, vigorous, educated. Seized on an alien world and transformed against his will into something monstrous. Burris was distressed by what had become of himself, naturally. A lesser man would have shattered. Burris had merely bent. That was interesting and praiseworthy, Chalk knew, in terms of what the public could gain from the story of Minner Burris. But Burris also suffered. That was interesting in Chalk's own terms.

Lona Kelvin. Girl. Orphaned early, a ward of the state. Not pretty, but of course her years of maturity were still ahead of her and she might ripen. Insecure, badly oriented toward men, and not very bright. (Or was she brighter than she dared let herself seem to be, Chalk wondered?) She had a thing in common with Burris. Scientists had seized upon her, too: not grisly alien Things, but kindly, benevolent, impartial high-order abstractions in white lab smocks, who without injuring Lona in any way had merely borrowed some unnecessary objects stored within her body and had used them in an experiment. That was all. And now Lona's hundred babies were sprouting in their gleaming plastic wombs. Had sprouted? Yes. Born already. Leaving a certain vacuum within Lona. She suffered.

29

It would be an act of charity, Duncan Chalk decided, to bring this suffering pair together.

'Send Bart in here,' he said to his chair.

Aoudad entered at once, as though rolling in on wheels, as though he had waited tensely in an anteroom for just this summons. He was gratifyingly tense. Long ago Aoudad had been self-sufficient and emotionally agile, but he had broken down, Chalk knew, under the lengthy strain. His compulsive womanizing was a clue to that. Yet to look at him, one saw the pretense of strength. The cool eyes, the firm lips. Chalk felt the subsurface emanations of fear and edginess. Aoudad waited.

Chalk said, 'Bart, can you bring Burris to see me right away?'

'He hasn't left his room in weeks.'

'I know that. But it's futile if I go to him. He's got to be coaxed back into public. I've decided to go ahead with the project.'

Aoudad radiated a kind of terror. 'I'll visit him, sir. I've been planning techniques of contact for some while. I'll offer incentives. He'll come.'

'Don't mention the girl to him just yet.'

'No. Certainly not.'

'You'll handle this well, Bart. I can rely on you. You know that. There's a great deal at stake, but you'll do your usually fine job.'

Chalk smiled. Aoudad smiled. On one, the smile was a weapon. On the other a defense. Chalk sensed the emanations. Deep within him, ductless glands were triggered, and he responded to Aoudad's uneasiness with a jolt of pleasure. Behind Aoudad's cool gray eyes uncertainties revolved. Yet Chalk had spoken the truth: he *did* have faith in Aoudad's skill in this matter. Only Aoudad himself did not have faith; and so Chalk's reassurances twisted the blade a trifle. Chalk had learned such tactics early.

Chalk said, 'Where's Nick?'

'Out. I think he's tracking that girl.'

'He nearly blundered last night. The girl was in the Arcade and wasn't properly protected. Some fool fingered her. Nick was lucky the girl resisted. I'm saving her.'

'Yes. Of course.'

'Naturally, no one recognized her. She's forgotten. Her year was last year, and today she's nothing. Still,' Chalk said, 'there's a good story in her, properly handled. And if some

30

ignorant grease gets his hands on her and stains her, it ruins the story. Nick should watch her more closely. I'll tell him that. You see about Burris.'

Aoudad quickly left the room. Chalk sat humming idly, enjoying himself. This thing would work. The public would love it when the romance flowered. There'd be money to reap. Of course, Chalk had little need for further money. It had motivated him once, but not now. Nor did the acquisition of greater power please him much. Despite the customary theories, Chalk had attained sufficient power so that he was willing to stop expanding if only he could be sure of holding what he had. No, it was something else, something inner, that governed his decisions now. When the love of money and the love of power are both sated, the love of love remains. Chalk did not find his love where others might find it, but he had his needs. Minner Burris and Lona Kelvin could fill those needs, perhaps. Catalysis. Synergy. Then he would see.

He closed his eyes.

He saw himself naked, afloat, gliding through the blue-green sea. Lofty waves buffeted his sleek white sides. His vast bulk moved easily, for it was weightless here, supported by the bosom of ocean, the bones for once not bowed by gravity's pull. Chalk was swift here. He wheeled to and fro, displaying his agility in the water. About him played dolphins, squid, marlin. Alongside him moved the solemn, stupid upright mass of a sunfish, no midget itself but dwarfed by his shining immensity.

Chalk saw boats on the horizon. Men coming toward him, upraised, grim-faced. He was quarry now. He laughed a thundering laugh. As the boats approached, he turned and swam toward them, teasing them, inviting them to do their worst. He was near the surface, gleaming whitely in the mid-day light. Sheets of water cascaded from his back.

Now the boats were near. Chalk pivoted. Mighty flukes lashed the water; a boat sprang high, became matchsticks, dumped its flailing cargo of men in the brine. A surge of muscle carried him away from his pursuers. He blew a great spouting geyser to celebrate his triumph. Then he plunged, sounding joyously, seeking the depths, and in moments his whiteness vanished into a realm where light was not free to enter.

Six

Moder Merci; Let Me Deye

'You should go out of your room,' the visitation suggested gently. 'Show yourself to the world. Meet it head on. There's nothing to fear.'

Burris groaned. 'You again! Won't you leave me alone?'

'How can I ever leave you?' his other self asked.

Burris stared through layers of gathering darkness. He had fed himself three times this day, so perhaps it was night, though he did not know and did not care. A gleaming slot provided him with any food he requested. The rearrangers of his body had improved his digestive system but had not made any fundamental changes in it. A small enough blessing, he felt; yet he still could cope with Earthside food. God knew where his enzymes now came from, but they were the same enzymes. Rennin, pepsin, the lipases, pancreatic amylase, trypsin, ptyalin, the whole diligent crew. What of the small intestine? What the fate of duodenum, jejunum, and ileum? What had replaced the mesentery and the peritoneum? Gone, gone, all gone, but rennin and pepsin somehow did their work. So the Earthside doctors who had examined him had said. Burris sensed that they would gladly dissect him to learn his secrets in more detail.

But not yet. Not just yet. He was coming toward that pass, but it would be a while.

And the apparition of former felicity would not absent itself.

'Look at your face,' Burris said. 'Your eyelids move so stupidly, up, down, blink, blink. The eyes are so crude. Your nose admits garbage to your throat. I must admit I'm a considerable improvement over you.'

'Of course. That's why I say go out, let yourself be admired by humanity.'

'When did humanity ever admire improved models of itself? Did Pithecanthropus fawn on the first Neanderthals? Did Neanderthal applaud the Aurignacians?'

'The analogy isn't proper. You didn't evolve past them, Minner. You were changed by external means. They have no reason to hate you for what you are.'

32

'They don't need to hate. Only to stare. Besides, I'm in pain. It's easier to remain here.'

'Is the pain really so hard to bear?'

'I grow accustomed to it,' Burris said. 'Yet every motion stabs me. The Things were only experimenting. They made their little mistakes. This extra chamber of my heart: whenever it contracts, I feel it in my throat. This shiny and permeable gut of mine: it passes food and I ache. I should kill myself. It's the best release.'

'Seek your comfort in literature,' the apparition counseled. 'Read. You once did. You were quite a well-read man, Minner. Three thousand years of literature at your command. Several languages. Homer. Chaucer. Shakespeare.'

Burris looked at the serene face of the man he had been. He recited: *'Moder, merci; let me deye.'*

'Finish it.'

'The rest's not applicable.'

'Finish it anyway.'

Burris said:

'For Aram ut of helle beye
And manken that is forloren.'

'Die, then,' the visitation said mildly. 'To buy Adam out of hell and mankind that is lost. Otherwise remain alive. Minner, do you think you're Jesus?'

'He suffered at the hands of strangers.'

'To redeem them. Will you redeem the Things if you go back to Manipool and die on their doorstep?'

Burris shrugged. 'I'm no redeemer. I need redeeming myself. I'm in a bad way.'

'Whining again!'

'Sune, I se thi bodi swungin.
thi brest, thin hond, thi fot thurch-stungen.'

Burris scowled. His new face was well designed for scowling; the lips rippled outward, like a sphincter door irising, baring the subdivided palisade of imperishable teeth. 'What do you want of me?' he asked.

'What do *you* want, Minner?'

'To put off this flesh. To have my old body back.'

'A miracle, that is. And you want the miracle to happen to you within these four walls.'

'As good a place as any. As likely as any.'

'No. Go outside. Seek help.'

'I've been outside. I've been prodded and poked. Not helped.

What shall I do – sell myself to a museum? Go away, you damned ghost. Out! Out!'

'Your redeemer liveth,' said the apparition.

'Tell me his address.'

No answer came. Burris found himself staring at cobwebbed shadows. The room purred with silence. Restlessness throbbed at him. His body now was designed to maintain tonus despite all idleness; it was a perfect spacefarer's body, equipped to drift from star to star, enduring all the long silence.

So had he drifted to Manipool. It lay on his route. Man was a newcomer among the stars, hardly having left his own planets behind. There was no telling what one would meet out there and what would happen to one. Burris had been the unlucky one. He had survived. The others lay in cheerful graves under a speckled sun. The Italians, Malcondotto and Prolisse – they had not come out of surgery. They were trial runs for Manipool's masterpiece, himself. Burris had seen Malcondotto, dead, after they had finished with him. He was at peace. He had looked so tranquil, if a monster can seem tranquil even in death. Prolisse had preceded him. Burris had not seen what they had done to Prolisse, and it had been just as well.

He had gone to the stars as a civilized man, alert, flexible of mind. No tubemonkey, no deckswabber. An officer, the highest product of mankind, armed with the higher mathematics and the highest topology. Mind stuffed with literary nuggets. A man who had loved, who had learned. Burris was glad now that he had never married. It is awkward for a starman to take a wife, but it is far more awkward to return from the stars transformed and embrace a former darling.

The ghost was back. 'Consult Aoudad,' is advised. 'He'll lead you to help. He'll make you a whole man again.'

'Aoudad?'

'Aoudad.'

'I will not see him.'

Burris was in solitude once more.

He looked at his hands. Delicate, tapering fingers, essentially unchanged except for the prehensile tentacle they had grafted to the outer phalanx on each side. Another of their little amusements. They might have put a pair of such tentacles below his arms, for that would have been useful. Or given him a prehensile tail, making him at least as efficient a brachiator as a Brazilian monkey. But these two muscular ropy things, pencil-thick and three inches long, what good were they? They had broadened his hand, he noticed for the first time, so that it would accommodate the new digit without disturbing the proportions. Considerate of them. Burris discovered some new facet of his newness every day. He thought of the dead Malcondotto. He thought of the dead Prolisse. He thought of Aoudad. Aoudad? How could Aoudad help him in any conceivable way?

They had stretched him on a table, or the Manipool equivalent of a table, something dipping and uncertain. They had measured him. What had they checked? Temperature, pulse rate, blood pressure, peristalsis, pupil dilation, iodine uptake, capillary function, and how much else? They had put calipers to the salty film over his eyeballs. They had computed the volume of cell content in the seminal duct. They had searched out the pathways of neural excitation, so that they could be blocked.

Anesthesia. Successful!

Surgery.

Peel back the rind. Seek for pituitary, hypothalamus, thyroid. Calm the fluttering ventricles. Descend with tiny intangible scalpels to enter the passages. The body, Galen had suspected, was merely a bag of blood. Was there a circulatory system? Was there a circulation? On Manipool they had discovered the secrets of human construction in three easy lessons. Malcondotto, Prolisse, Burris. Two they had wasted. The third endured.

They had tied off blood vessels. They had exposed the gray silkiness of the brain. Here was the mode of Chaucer. Here Piers Plowman. Aggression here. Vindictiveness. Sensory perception. Charity. Faith. In this shining bulge dwelled Proust, Hemingway, Mozart, Beethoven. Rembrandt here.

See, see where Christ's blood streams in the firmament!

He had waited for it to begin, knowing that Malcondotto had perished under their ministrations and that Prolisse, flayed and diced, was gone. *Stand still, you ever-moving spheres of heaven, that time may cease and midnight never come.* Midnight came. The slithering knives dug at his brain. It would not hurt, he was sure of that, and yet he feared the pain. His only body, his irreplaceable self. He had not harmed them. He had come in innocence.

Once, in boyhood, he had cut his leg while playing, a deep cut gaping wide to reveal raw meat within. *A gash,* he thought, *I have a gash.* Blood had spouted over his feet. They had

35

healed it, not so swiftly as such things were done today, but as he watched the red slash knit, he had meditated on the change that had worked. His leg would never be the same again, for now it bore the cicatrix of injury. That had moved him profoundly, at twelve – so fundamental a change in his body, so permanent. He thought of that in the final moments before the Things began work on him. *Mountains and hills, come, come and fall on me, and hide me from the heavy wrath of God! No, no! Then will I headlong run into the earth: earth, gape!*

An idle command.

O, no, it will not harbour me!

The silent knives whirled. The nuclei of the medulla, receiving impulses from the vestibular mechanism of the ear – gone. The basal ganglia. The sulci and the gyri. The bronchi with their cartilaginous rings. The alveoli, the wondrous sponges. Epiglottis. Vas deferens. Lymphatic vessels. Dendrites and axons. The doctors were quite curious: how does this marvelous creature work? What composes him?

They unstrung him until he was spread out etherized on a table, extending an infinite distance. Was he still alive at that point? Bundles of nerves, bushels of intestine. *Now, body, turn to air, or Lucifer will bear thee quick to hell! O soul, be chang'd into little water-drops, and fall into the ocean, ne'er be found!*

Patiently they had restored him. Tediously did they reconstruct him, improving where minded on the original model. And then, no doubt in great pride, they of Manipool had returned him to his people.

Come not, Lucifer!

'Consult Aoudad,' the apparition advised.

Aoudad? *Aoudad?*

Seven

Here's Death, Twitching My Ear

The room stank. Its stink was vile. Wondering if the man ever troubled to ventilate, Bart Aoudad subtly introduced an olfactory depressant into his system. The brain would function as keenly as ever; it had better. But the nostrils would cease for the moment to report all they might.

He was lucky to be in here, stink or not. He had won the privilege through diligent courtship.

Burris said, 'Can you look at me?'

'Easily. You fascinate me, honestly. Did you expect me to be repelled?'

'Most people so far have been.'

'Most people are fools,' said Aoudad.

He did not reveal that he had monitored Burris for many weeks now, long enough to steel himself against the strangenesses of the man. Strange he was, and repellent enough; yet the configurations grew on one. Aoudad was not yet ready to apply for the same sort of beauty treatment, but he was numb to Burris's deformities.

'Can you help me?' Burris asked.

'I believe I can.'

'Provided I want help.'

'I assume that you do.'

Burris shrugged. 'I'm not certain of that. You might say I'm growing accustomed to my present appearance. In another few days I might start going outdoors again.'

It was a lie, Aoudad knew. Which one of them Burris was trying to delude, Aoudad could not positively say. But, however blandly Burris hid his bitterness at the moment, the visitor had ample knowledge that it still festered within him. Burris wanted out of this body.

Aoudad said, 'I am in the employ of Duncan Chalk. Do you know the name?'

'No.'

'But – ' Aoudad swallowed his surprise. 'Of course. You haven't spent much time on Earth. Chalk brings amusement to the world. Perhaps you've visited the Arcade, or maybe you've been to Luna Tivoli.'

'I know of them.'

'They are Chalk's enterprises. Among many others. He keeps billions of people happy in this system. He is even planning to expand to other systems shortly.' That was a bit of imaginative hyperbole on Aoudad's part, but Burris did not need to know it.

Burris said, 'So?'

'Chalk is wealthy, you see. Chalk is humanitarian. The combination is a good one. It holds possibilities that may benefit you.'

'I see them already,' said Burris smoothly, leaning forward and entwining the outer tentacles that squirmed on his hands. 'You hire me as an exhibit in Chalk's circuses. You pay me eight million a year. Every curiosity-seeker in the system comes to have his look. Chalk gets richer, I become a millionaire and die happy, and the petty curiosities of the multitudes are gratified. Yes?'

'No,' Aoudad said, alarmed by the nearness of Burris's guess. 'I'm sure you're merely joking. You must realize that Mr Chalk could not conceivably exploit your – ah – misfortune in such a way.'

'Do you think it's such a misfortune?' asked Burris. 'I'm quite efficient this way. Of course, there's pain, but I can stay underwater for fifteen minutes. Can you do that? Do you feel so sorry for me?'

I must not let him lead me astray, Aoudad resolved. He's devilish. He'd get along well with Chalk.

Aoudad said, 'Certainly I'm happy to know that you find your present situation reasonably satisfactory. Yet – let me be frank – I suspect you'd be glad to return to normal human form.'

'You think so, do you?'

'Yes.'

'You're a remarkably perceptive man, Mr Aoudad. Have you brought your magic wand?'

'There's no magic involved. But if you're willing to supply a quid for our quo, it's possible that Chalk can arrange to have you transferred to a more conventional body.'

The effect on Burris was immediate and electric.

He dropped the pose of casual indifference. He cast aside the mocking detachment behind which, Aoudad realized, he hid his agony. His body trembled like a glass flower strummed by the breeze. There was momentary loss of muscular control: the mouth convulsively flashed sidewise smiles, a flapping gate, and the shuttered eyes clicked a dozen times.

'How can this be done?' Burris demanded.

'Let Chalk explain it to you.'

Burris's hand dug into Aoudad's thigh. Aoudad did not shrink at the metallic touch.

Burris said hoarsely: 'Is it possible?'

'It may be. The technique is not perfected yet.'

'Am I to be the guinea pig this time, too?'

'Please. Chalk would not expose you to further distress. There will be additional research before the process can be applied to you. Will you talk to him?'

Hesitation. Once more eyes and mouth acted seemingly without Burris's volition. Then the starman regained command of himself. He straightened, twining his hands together, crossing his legs. How many knee-joints does he have, Aoudad wondered? Burris was silent. Calculating. Electrons surging down the pathways of that tormented brain.

Burris said, 'If Chalk can place me in another body – '

'Yes?'

'What will he gain from it?'

'I told you. Chalk's a humanitarian. He knows you're in pain. He wants to do something about it. See him, Burris. Let him help you.'

'Who are you, Aoudad?'

'No one. A limb of Duncan Chalk.'

'Is this a trap?'

'You're too suspicious,' Aoudad said. 'We mean the best for you.'

Silence. Burris rose, pacing the room in a peculiarly liquid gliding step. Aoudad was taut.

'To Chalk,' Burris murmured finally. 'Yes. Take me to Chalk!'

Eight

Stabat Mater Dolorosa

In the dark it was easy for Lona to pretend that she was dead.
She often mourned at her own grave. She saw herself on a
hillside, on a grassy breast of earth with a tiny plaque set in
the ground at her feet. HERE LIES.

VICTIM.

MURDERED BY SCIENTISTS.

She drew the coverlets up over her thin body. Her eyes,
tightly closed, held back the tears. BLESSED REPOSE. HOPE
OF REDEMPTION. What did they do with dead bodies nowadays? Pop them in the oven! A bright hot flash. Light, like the
sun. And then dust. Dust to dust. A long sleep.

I was nearly dead once, Lona reminded herself. But they
stopped me. They brought me back.

Six months ago, in the full blaze of summer. A good season
for dying, Lona thought. Her babies had been born. It didn't
take nine months, the way they did it, bringing them along in
bottles. More like six months. The experiment had taken place
exactly a year back. Six months for the babies to hatch. Then
the unbearable publicity – and the brush with deliberate death.

Why had they chosen her?

Because she was there. Because she was available. Because
she could not object. Because she carried a bellyful of fertile
eggs that she wasn't likely ever to need.

'A woman's ovaries contain several hundred thousand ova,
Miss Kelvin. During your normal lifetime about four hundred of these will reach maturity. The rest are superfluous.
These are the ones we wish to use. We need only a few hundred ...'

'In the name of science ...'

'A crucial experiment ...'

'The ova are superfluous. You can dispense with them and
feel no loss ...'

'Medical history ... your name ... forever ...'

'No effect on your future fertility. You can marry and have
a dozen normal children ...'

It was an intricate experiment with many facets. They had had a century or so to perfect the techniques, and now they were bringing them all together in a single project. Natural oögenesis coupled with synthetic ripening of the ova. Embryonic induction. External fertilization. Extramaternal incubation after reimplanting of fertilized ova. Words. Sounds. Synthetic capacitation. *Ex utero* fetal development. Simultaneity of genetic material. My babies! My babies!

Lona did not know who the 'father' was, only that a single donor would contribute all of the sperm, just as a single donor would contribute all of the ova. She understood that much. The doctors were very good about explaining the project to her, step by step, speaking to her as they would to a child. She followed most of it. They patronized her because she had had no education to speak of and because she was timid of embracing tough ideas, but the raw intelligence was there.

Her part in the project was simple and ended at the first phase. They flushed from her ovaries several hundred fertile but immature eggs. So far as they were concerned, Lona could then drop into outer darkness. But she had to know. She followed the subsequent steps.

The eggs were coddled along in artificial ovaries until they were ripe. A woman could ripen only two or three ova at a time in the hidden greenhouse of her middle; the machines could and did handle hundreds. Came then the taxing but not essentially new process of microinjection of the eggs to strengthen them. And then fertilization. The swimming sperms wriggled toward their goal. A single donor, a single explosive burst at harvest-time. Many ova had been lost in the earlier stages. Many were not fertile or not fertilized. But a hundred were. The tiny wriggler reached its harbor.

Reimplantation of the fertilized ova now. There had been talk of finding a hundred other women to carry the hundred sprouting zygotes. Cuckoo fetuses, swelling the wrong bellies. In the end, though, that was considered excessive. A dozen women volunteered to carry to term; the rest of the fertilized ova went to the artificial wombs. A dozen pale bellies bare under the bright lights. A dozen pairs of smooth thighs opening not to a lover but to dull gray aluminum sheathing. The slow thrust, the squirting entry, the completion of implantation. Some attempts were failures. Eight of the sleek bellies soon were bulging.

41

'Let me volunteer,' Lona had said. Touching her flat belly: 'Let me carry one of the babies.'

'No.'

They were gentler than that. They explained that it was unnecessary within the framework of the experiment for her to go through the bother of pregnancy. It had been shown long ago that an ovum could be taken from a woman's body, fertilized elsewhere, and reimplanted in her for the usual term of nurture. Why repeat? That had been verified, confirmed. She could be spared the nuisance. They wished to know how well a human mother carried an intrusive embryo, and for that they did not need Lona.

Did anyone need Lona now?

No one needed Lona now.

No one. Lona paid heed to what was happening.

The eight volunteer mothers did well. In them pregnancy was artificially accelerated. Their bodies accepted the intruders, fed blood to them, folded them warmly in placentas. A medical miracle, yes. But how much more exciting to dispense with maternity altogether!

A row of gleaming boxes. In each a dividing zygote. The pace of cell-splitting was breathtaking. Lona's head reeled. Growth was induced in the cortical cytoplasm of the zygotes as they cleaved, then in the main axial organs. 'As gastrulation proceeds, the mesodermal mantle extends forward from the blastopore, and its anterior edge comes to lie just posterior to the future lens ectoderm. This edge is the future heart, and it, too, is an inductor of the lens. At the open-neuralplate stage of development, the future lens cells are located in two areas of the epidermis that lie just lateral to the anterior brain plate. As the neural plate rolls up into a tube, the future retinal cells evaginate from the prospective brain as part of the optic vesicle.'

In six months a hundred bouncing babies.

A word never before used in a human context now on the lips of all: *centuplets*.

Why not? One mother, one father! The rest was incidental. The carrier women, the metal wombs – they had lent warmth and sustenance, but they were not mothers to the children.

Who was the mother?

The father did not matter. Artificial insemination was a matter for yawns. Statistically, at least, one male could fertilize every woman in the world in two afternoons. If a man's sperm

42

had spawned a hundred babies at once, what of it?

But the *mother* . . .

Her name was not supposed to be released. 'Anonymous donor' – that was her place in medical history. The story was too good, though. Especially that she was not quite seventeen. Especially that she was single. Especially that (so the physicians swore) she was technically virgin.

Two days after the simultaneous centuplet delivery, Lona's name and achievement were matters of public record.

She stood slim and frightened before the flashing lights.

'Will you name the babies yourself?'

'What did it feel like when the eggs were taken from you?'

'What does it feel like to know that you're the mother of the biggest family in human history?'

'Will you marry me?'

'Come live with me and be my love.'

'Half a million for the exclusive rights to the story!'

'*Never* with a man?'

'How did you react when they told you what the experiment was going to be?'

'Have you met the father?'

'   '

A month like that. Fair skin reddened by camera-glow. Eyes wide, strained, bloodshot. Questions. Doctors beside her to guide her answers. Her moment of glory, dazzling, bewildering. The doctors hated it nearly as much as she did. They would never have released her name: except that one of them had, for a price, and the floodgates had opened. Now they tried to ward off more blunders by coaching her in what to say. Lona said quite little, actually. Part of her silence rose from fright, part from ignorance. What could she tell the world? What did the world want from her?

Briefly she was a wonder of the world. They sang a song about her on the song machines. Deep thrumming of chords; sad lament of the mother of centuplets. It was played everywhere. She could not bear to listen. Come make a baby with me, sweetie. Come make a hundred more. Her friends, not many of them to begin with, sensed that it embarrassed her to talk of It, so they talked deliberately of other things, anything else at all, and finally they simply stopped talking. She kept to herself. Strangers wanted to know what it was like, with all those babies. How could she say? She scarcely knew! Why had

43

they made a song about her? Why did they gossip and pry? What did they *want*?

To some, it was all blasphemy. There was thunder from the pulpits. Lona felt the tang of brimstone at her nostrils. The babies cried and stretched and gurgled. She visited them once, and wept, and picked one up to hug it. The child was taken from her and restored to its aseptic environment. She was not permitted to visit them again.

Centuplets. A hundred siblings sharing the same group of codons. What would they be like? How would they grow? Could a man live in a world shared by fifty brothers and fifty sisters? That was part of the experiment. This experiment was to be a lifetime long. The psychologists had moved in. Much was known of quintuplets: sextuplets had been studied somewhat, and there had briefly been a set of septuplets thirty years before. But centuplets? An infinity of new research!

Without Lona. Her part had ended on the first day. Something cool and tingly swabbed across her thighs by a smiling nurse. Then men, staring without interest at her body. A drug. A dreamy haze through which she was aware of penetration. No other sensation. The end. 'Thank you, Miss Kelvin. Your fee.' Cool linens against her body. Elsewhere they were beginning to do things to the borrowed ova.

My babies. My babies.

Lights in my eyes!

When the time came to kill herself, Lona did not quite succeed at it. Doctors who could give life to a speck of matter could also sustain life in the source of that speck. They put her back together, and then they forgot about her.

A nine days' wonder is granted obscurity on the tenth day.

Obscurity, but not peace. Peace was never granted; it had to be won, the hard way, from within. Living again in darkness, Lona yet could never be the same, for somewhere else a hundred babies thrived and fattened. They had reached not only into her ovaries but into the fabric of her life itself to draw forth those babies, and she reverberated still with the recoil.

She shivered in the darkness.

Someday soon, she promised herself, I'll try again. And this time no one will notice me. This time they'll let me go. I'll sleep a long time.

Nine

In the Beginning was the Word

For Burris it was something like being born. He had not left his room in so many weeks that it had come to seem a permanent shelter.

Aoudad thoughtfully made the delivery as painless as possible for him, though. They left at dead of night, when the city slept. Burris was cloaked and hooded. It gave him such a conspiratorial look that he was forced to smile at the effect; yet he regarded it as necessary. The hood hid him well, and so long as he kept his head down, he was safe from the glances of the casual. As they left the building, Burris remained in the far corner of the dropshaft, praying that no one else would summon it as he descended. No one did. But on the way through the entrance, a drifting blob of glowing light illuminated him for a moment just when a homecoming resident appeared. The man paused, staring beneath the hood. Burris remained expressionless. The man blinked, seeing the unexpected. Burris's harsh, distorted face regarded him coldly, and the man moved on. His sleep would be tinctured with nightmare that night. But that was better, thought Burris, than having the nightmare steal into the texture of your life itself, as had happened to him.

A car waited just beyond the lip of the building.

'Chalk doesn't ordinarily hold interviews at this hour,' Aoudad chattered. 'But you must understand that this is something special. He means to give you every consideration.'

'Splendid,' Burris said darkly.

They entered the car. It was like exchanging one womb for another less spacious but more inviting. Burris settled against a couch-seat big enough for several people, but evidently modeled to fit a single pair of enormous buttocks. Aoudad sat beside him in a more normal accommodation. The car started, gliding quietly away in a thrum of turbines. Its transponders picked up the emanations of the nearest highway, and shortly they left city streets behind and were hurtling along a restricted-access route.

45

The windows of the car were comfortingly opaque. Burris threw back the hood. He was accustoming himself in short stages to showing himself to other people. Aoudad, who did not appear to mind his mutilations, was a good subject on whom to practice.

'Drink?' Aoudad asked. 'Smoke? Any kind of stimulant?'

'Thank you, no.'

'Are you able to touch such things – the way you are?'

Burris smiled grimly. 'My metabolism is basically the same as yours, even now. The plumbing's different. I eat your food. I drink your drinks. But not right this moment.'

'I wondered. You'll pardon my curiosity.'

'Of course.'

'And the bodily functions –'

'They've improved excretion. I don't know what they've done to reproduction. The organs are still there, but do they function? It's not a test I've cared to make.'

The muscles of Aoudad's left cheek pulled back as though in a spasm. The response was not lost on Burris. Why is he so interested in my sex life? Normal prurience? Something more?

'You'll pardon my curiosity,' Aoudad said again.

'I already have.' Burris leaned back and felt his seat doing odd things to him. A massage, perhaps. No doubt he was tense and the poor chair was trying to fix things. But the chair was programmed for a bigger man. It seemed to be humming as if with an overloaded circuit. Was it troubled just by the size differential, Burris wondered? Or did the restructured contours of his anatomy cause it some distress?

He mentioned the chair to Aoudad, who cut it off. Smiling, Burris complimented himself on his state of mellowed relaxation. He had not said a bitter thing since Aoudad's arrival. He was calm, tempest-free, hovering at dead center. Good. Good. He had spent too much time alone, letting his miseries corrode him. This fool Aoudad was an angel of mercy come to lift him out of himself. I am grateful, said Burris pleasantly to himself.

'This is it. Chalk's office is here.'

The building was relatively low, no more than three or four storeys, but it was well set off from the towers that flanked it. Its sprawling horizontal bulk compensated for its lack of height. Wide-legged angles stretched off to right and left; Burris, making useful use of his added peripheral vision, peered as far as he could around the sides of the building and calculated that it was probably eight-sided. The outer wall was

46

of a dull brown metal, neatly finished, pebbled in an ornamental way. No light was visible within; but, then, there were no windows.

One wall abruptly gaped at them as a hidden portcullis silently lifted. The car rocketed through and came to a halt in the bowels of the building. Its hatch sprang off. Burris became aware that a short bright-eyed man was peering into the car at him.

He experienced a moment of shock at finding himself so unexpectedly being viewed by a stranger. Then he recovered and reversed the flow of the sensation, staring back. The short man was worth staring at, too. Without the benefit of malevolent surgeons, he was nonetheless strikingly ugly. Virtually neckless; thick matted dark hair descending into his collar; large jug ears; a narrow-bridged nose; incredible long, thin lips that just now were puckered in a repellent pout of fascination. No beauty.

Aoudad said: 'Minner Burris. Leontes d'Amore. Of the Chalk staff.'

'Chalk's awake. He's waiting,' said d'Amore. Even his voice was ugly.

Yet he faces the world every day, Burris reflected.

Hooded once more, he let himself be swept along a network of pneumatic tubes until he found himself gliding into an immense cavernous room studded with various levels of activity-points. Just now there was little activity; the desks were empty, the screens were silent. A gentle glow of thermo-luminescent fungi lit the place. Turning slowly, Burris panned his gaze across the room and up a series of crystal rungs until he observed, seated thronewise near the ceiling on the far side, a vast individual.

Chalk. Obviously.

Burris stood absorbed in the sight, forgetting for a moment the million tiny pricking pains that were his constant companions. So big? So enfleshed? The man had devoured a legion of cattle to gain that bulk.

Besides him, Aoudad gently urged him forward, not quite daring to touch Burris's elbow.

'Let me see you,' Chalk said. His voice was light, amiable. 'Up to me, Burris.'

A moment more. Face to face.

Buriss shrugged off the hood and then the cloak. Let him have his look. Before this mound of flesh I need feel no shame.

47

Chalk's placid expression did not change.

He studied Burris carefully, with deep interest and no hint of revulsion. At a wave of his pudgy hand, Aoudad and d'Amore vanished. Burris and Chalk remained alone in the huge, dim room.

'They did quite a job on you,' Chalk remarked. 'Do you have any idea why they did it?'

'Sheer curiosity. Also the desire to improve. In their inhuman way, they're quite human.'

'What do they look like?'

'Pockmarked. Leathery. I'd rather not say.'

'All right.' Chalk had not risen. Burris stood before him, hands folded, the little outer tentacles twining and untwining. He sensed a seat behind him and took it unbidden.

'You have quite a place here,' he said.

Chalk smiled and let the statement roll away. He said, 'Does it hurt?'

'What?'

'Your changes.'

'There's considerable discomfort. Terran painkillers don't help much. They did things to the neural channels, and no one here knows quite where to apply the blocks. But it's bearable. They say the limbs of amputees throb for years after they've been removed. Same sensation, I guess.'

'Were any of your limbs removed?'

'All of them,' Burris said. 'And put back on again a new way. The medics who examined me were very pleased by my joints. Also my tendons and ligaments. These are my own original hands, a little altered. My feet. I'm not really sure how much else of me is mine and how much theirs.'

'And internally?'

'All different. Chaos. A report is being prepared. I haven't been back on Earth long. They studied me awhile, and then I rebelled.'

'Why?'

'I was becoming a thing. Not only to them but to myself. I'm not a thing. I'm a human being who's been rearranged. Inside, I'm still human. Prick me and I'll bleed. What can you do for me, Chalk?'

A meaty hand waved. 'Patience. Patience. I want to know more about you. You were a space officer?'

'Yes.'

'Academy and all?'

48

'Naturally.'

'Your rating must have been good. You were given a tough assignment. First landing on a world of intelligent beings – never a cinch. How many in your team?'

'Three. We all went through surgery. Prolisse died first, then Malcondotto. Lucky for them.'

'You dislike your present body?'

'It has its advantages. The doctors say I'm likely to live five hundred years. But it's painful, and it's also embarrassing. I was never cut out to be a monster.'

'You're not as ugly as you may think you are,' Chalk observed. 'Oh, yes, children run screaming from you, that sort of thing. But children are conservatives. They loathe anything new. I find that face of yours quite attractive in its way. I daresay a lot of women would fling themselves at your feet.'

'I don't know. I haven't tried.'

'Grotesqueness has its appeal, Burris. I weighed over twenty pounds at birth. My weight has never hampered me. I think of it as an asset.'

'You've had a lifetime to get used to your size,' said Burris. 'You accommodate to it in a thousand ways. Also, you chose to be this way. I was the victim of an incomprehensible whim. It's a violation. I've been raped, Chalk.'

'You want it all undone?'

'What do you think?'

Chalk nodded. His eyelids slid down, and it appeared that he had dropped instantly into a sound sleep. Burris waited, baffled, and more than a minute passed. Without stirring, Chalk said, 'Surgeons here on Earth can transplant brains successfully from one body to another.'

Burris started, seized by a *grand mal* of fevered excitement. A new organ within his body injected spurts of some unknown hormone into the bowl of strangenesses beside his heart. He dizzied. He scrabbled in the rolling surf, dashed again and again onto the abrasive sand by relentless waves.

Chalk went on calmly, 'Does the technology of the thing interest you at all?'

The tentacles of Burris's hands writhed uncontrollably.

The smooth words came: 'The brain must be surgically isolated within the skull by paring away of all contiguous tissues. The cranium itself is preserved for support and protection. Naturally, absolute hemostasis must be maintained during the long period of anticoagulation, and there are techniques

4 49

for sealing the base of the skull and the frontal bone to prevent loss of blood. Brain functions are monitored by electrodes and thermoprobes. Circulation is maintained by linking the internal maxillary and internal carotid arteries. Vascular loops, you understand. I'll spare you the details by which the body is shaved away, leaving only the living brain. At length the spinal cord is severed and the brain is totally isolated, fed by its own carotid system. Meanwhile the recipient has been prepared. The carotid and jugular are dissected away and the major strap muscles in the cervical area are resected. The brain graft is put in place after submergence in an antibiotic solution. The carotid arteries of the isolated brain are connected by a siliconized cannula to the proximal carotid artery of the recipient. A second cannula is fixed in the jugular of the recipient. All this is done in a low freeze to minimize damage. Once the grafted brain's circulation is meshed with that of the recipient body, we bring the temperature toward normal and begin standard post-operative techniques. A prolonged period of re-education is necessary before the grafted brain has assumed control over the recipient body.'

'Remarkable.'

'Not much of an achievement compared with what was done to you,' Chalk conceded. 'But it's been carried out successfully with higher mammals. Even with primates.'

'With humans?'

'No.'

'Then –'

'Terminal patients have been used. Brains grafted into recently deceased. Too much goes against the chance of success there, though. Still, there have been some near misses. Another three years, Burris, and human beings will be swapping brains as easily as they swap arms and legs today.'

Burris disliked the sensations of intense anticipation that roared through him. His skin temperature was uncomfortably high. His throat throbbed.

Chalk said, 'We build a synthetic for you, duplicating in as many respects as possible your original appearance. We assemble a golem, you see, from the spare-parts bank, but we do not include a brain. We transplant your brain into the assemblage. There will be differences, naturally, but you'll be fundamentally integral. Interested?'

'Don't torture me, Chalk.'

'I give you my word I'm serious. Two technological problems stand in the way. We have to master the techniques of total assembly of a recipient, and we have to keep it alive until we can successfully carry out the transplant. I've already said it would take three years to achieve the second. Say two more to build the golem. Five years, Burris, and you'll be fully human again.'

'What will this cost?'

'Perhaps a hundred million. Perhaps more.'

Burris laughed harshly. His tongue – how like a serpent's now! – flickered into view.

Chalk: 'I'm prepared to underwrite the entire cost of your rehabilitation.'

'You're dealing in fantasy now.'

'I ask you to have faith in my resources. Are you willing to part with your present body if I can supply something closer to the human norm?'

It was a question that Burris had never expected anyone to ask him. He was startled by the extent of his own vacillation. He detested this body and was bowed beneath the weight of the thing that had been perpetrated on him. And yet, was he coming to love his alienness?

He said after a brief pause, 'The sooner I could shed this thing, the better.'

'Good. Now, there's the problem of your getting through the five years or so that this will take. I propose that we attempt to modify your facial appearance, at least, so that you'll be able to get along in society until we can make the switch. Does that interest you?'

'It can't be done. I've already explored the idea with the doctors who examined me after my return. I'm a mess of strange antibodies, and I'll reject any graft.'

'Do you think that's so? Or were they merely telling you a convenient lie?'

'I think it's so.'

'Let me send you to a hospital,' Chalk suggested. 'We'll run a few tests to confirm the earlier verdict. If it's so, so. If not, we can make life a little easier for you. Yes?'

'Why are you doing this, Chalk? What's the quid pro quo?'

The fat man pivoted and swung ponderously forward until his eyes were only inches from Burris's face. Burris surveyed the oddly delicate lips, the fine nose, the immense cheeks and puffy eyelids. In a low voice Chalk murmured, 'The price is a

51

steep one. It'll sicken you to the core. You'll turn down the whole deal.'

'What is it?'

'I'm a purveyor of popular amusement. I can't remotely get my investment back out of you, but I want to recover what I can.'

'The price?'

'Full rights to commercial exploitation of your story,' said Chalk. 'Beginning with your seizure by the aliens, carrying through your return to Earth and your difficult adjustment to your altered condition, and continuing on through your forth-coming period of re-adaptation. The world already knows that three men came to a planet called Manipool, two were killed, and a third came back the victim of surgical experiments. That much was announced, and then you dropped from sight. I want to put you back in sight. I want to show you redis-covering your humanity, relating to other people again, groping upward out of hell, eventually triumphing over your cata-strophic experience and coming out of it purged. It'll mean a frequent intrusion on your privacy, and I'm prepared to hear you refuse. After all, one would expect – '

'It's a new form of torture, is it?'

'Something of an ordeal, perhaps,' Chalk admitted. His wide forehead was stippled with sweat. He looked flushed and strained, as though approaching some sort of inner emotional climax.

'Purged,' Burris whispered. 'You offer me purgatory.'

'Call it that.'

'I hide for weeks. Then I stand naked before the universe for five years. Eh?'

'Expenses paid.'

'Expenses paid,' said Burris. 'Yes. Yes. I accept the torture. I'm your toy, Chalk. Only a human being would refuse the offer. But I accept. I accept!'

Ten

A Pound of Flesh

'He's at the hospital,' Aoudad said. 'They've begun to study him.' He plucked at the woman's clothes. 'Take them off, Elise.'

Elise Prolisse brushed the questing hand away. 'Will Chalk really put him back in a human body?'

'I don't doubt it.'

'Then if Marco had returned alive, he might have been put back, too.'

Aoudad was noncommittal. 'You're dealing in too many ifs now. Marco's dead. Open your robe, dear.'

'Wait. Can I visit Burris in the hospital?'

'I suppose. What do you want with him?'

'Just to talk. He was the last man to see my husband alive, remember? He can tell me how Marco died.'

'You would not want to know,' said Aoudad softly. 'Marco died as they tried to make him into the kind of creature Burris now is. If you saw Burris, you would realize that Marco is better off dead.'

'All the same – '

'You would not want to know.'

'I asked to see him,' Elise said dreamily, 'as soon as he returned. I wanted to talk to him about Marco. And the other, Malcondotto – he had a widow, too. But they would not let us near him. And afterward Burris disappeared. You could take me to him!'

'It's for your own good that you keep away,' Aoudad told her. His hands crept up her body, lingering, seeking out the magnetic snaps and depolarizing them. The garment opened. The heavy breasts came into view, deathly white, tipped with circlets of deep red. He felt the inward stab of desire. She caught his hands as he reached for them.

'You will help me see Burris?' she asked.

'I – '

'You will help me see Burris.' Not a question this time.

'Yes. Yes.'

The hands blocking his path dropped away. Trembling, Aoudad peeled back the garments. She was a handsome woman, past her first youth, meaty, yet handsome. These Italians! White skin, dark hair. *Sensualissima!* Let her see Burris if she wished. Would Chalk object? Chalk had already indicated the kind of matchmaking he expected. Burris and the Kelvin girl. But perhaps Burris and the widow Prolisse first? Aoudad's mind churned.

Elise looked up at him in adoration as his lean, tough body poised above her.

Her last garment surrendered. He stared at acres of whiteness, islands of black and red.

'Tomorrow you will arrange it,' she said.

'Yes. Tomorrow.'

He fell upon her nakedness. Around the fleshy part of her left thigh she wore a black velvet band. A mourning band for Marco Prolisse, done to death incomprehensibly by incomprehensible beings on an incomprehensible world. *Pover'uomo!* Her flesh blazed. She was incandescent. A tropical valley beckoned to him. Aoudad entered. Almost at once came a strangled cry of ecstasy.

Eleven
Two if by Night

The hospital lay at the very edge of the desert. It was a U-shaped building, long and low, whose limbs pointed toward the east. Early sunlight, rising, crept along them until it splashed against the long horizontal bar linking the parallel vertical wings. The construction was of gray sandstone tinged with red. Just to the west of the building – that is, behind its main section – was a narrow garden strip, and beyond the garden began the zone of dry brownish desert.

The desert was not without life of its own. Somber tufts of sagebrush were common. Beneath the parched surface were the tunnels of rodents. Kangaroo mice could be seen by the lucky at night, grasshoppers during the day. Cacti and euphorbias and other succulents studded the earth.

Some of the desert's abundant life had invaded the hospital grounds themselves. The garden in the rear was a desert garden, thick with the thorned things of dryness. The courtyard between the two limbs of the U had been planted with cacti also. Here stood a saguaro six times the height of a man, with rugged central trunk and five skyward arms. There, framing it, were two speciments of the bizarre variant form, the cancer cactus, solid trunk, two small arms crying help, and a cluster of gnarled, twisted growths at the summit. Down the path, three-high, the grotesque white cholla. Facing it, squat, sturdy, the thorn-girdled barrel of a water cactus. Spiny canes of an opuntia; flat grayish pads of the prickly pear; looping loveliness of a cereus. At other times of the year these formidable, bristling, stolid gargoyles bore tender blossoms, yellow and violet and pink, pale and delicate. But this was winter. The air was dry, the sky blue in a hard way and cloudless, though snow never fell here. This was a timeless place, the humidity close to zero. The winds could be chilling, free of weather, going through a fifty-degree shift of temperature from summer to winter but otherwise remaining unaltered.

This was the place to which Lona Kelvin had been brought in summer, six months ago, after her attempt at suicide. Most of the cacti had already flowered by then. Now she was back, and she had missed the flowering season once more, coming three months too soon instead of three months too late. It would have been better for her to time her self-destructive impulses more precisely.

The doctors stood above her bed, speaking of her as though she were elsewhere.

'It'll be easier to repair her this time. No need to heal bones. Just a lung graft or so and she'll be all right.'

'Until she tries again.'

'That's not for me to worry about. Let them send her for psychotherapy. All I do is repair the shattered body.'

'Not shattered just now, though. Just badly used.'

'She'll get herself sooner or later. A really determined self-destroyer always succeeds. Let them step into nuclear converters, or something permanent like that. Jump from ninety floors up. We can't paste a smear of molecules together.'

'Aren't you afraid you'll give her ideas?'

'If she's listening. But she could have thought of that herself if she wanted to.'

'You've got something there. Maybe she's not a really determined self-destroyer. Maybe she's just a self-advertiser.'

'I think I agree. Two suicide attempts in six months, both of them botched – when all she needed to do was open the window and jump – '

'What's the alveolar count?'

'Not bad.'

'Her blood pressure?'

'Rising. Adrenocortical flow's down. Respiration up two points. She's coming along.'

'We'll have her walking in the desert in three days.'

'She'll need rest. Someone to talk to her. Why the hell does she want to be dead, anyway?'

'Who knows? I wouldn't think she was bright enough to want to kill herself.'

'Fear and trembling. The sickness unto death.'

'Anomie is supposedly reserved for more complex . . . '

They moved away from her bed, still talking. Lona did not open her eyes. She had not even been able to decide how many of them had been over her. Three, she guessed. More than two, less than four – so it had seemed. But their voices were so similar. And they didn't really argue with each other; they simply placed one slab of statement atop the next, gluing them carefully in place. Why had they saved her if they thought so little of her?

This time she had been certain she was going to die.

There are ways and ways of getting killed. Lona was shrewd enough to conceive of the most reliable ones, yet somehow had not permitted herself to try them, not out of fear of meeting death but out of fear of what she might encounter on the road. That other time she had hurled herself in front of a truck. Not on a highway, where vehicles hurtling toward her at a hundred and fifty miles an hour would swiftly and effectively mince her, but on a city street, where she was caught and tossed and slammed down, broken but not totally shattered, against the side of a building. So they had rebuilt her bones, and she had walked again in a month, and she was without outer scars.

And yesterday – it had seemed so simple to go down the hall to the dissolver room, and carefully disregard the rules by opening the disposal sac, and thrust her head in, and take a deep breath of the acrid fumes –

Throat and lungs and throbbing heart should have dissolved

56

away. Given an hour's time, as she lay twitching on the cold floor, and they would have. But within minutes Lona was in helpful hands. Forcing down her throat some neutralizing substance. Thrusting her into a car. The first-aid station. Then the hospital, a thousand miles from home.

She was alive.

She was injured, of course. She had burned her nasal passages, had damaged her throat, had lost a considerable chunk of lung tissue. They had repaired the minor damage last night, and already nose and throat were healing. In a few days her lungs would be whole again. Death had no dominion in this land any longer.

Pale sunlight caressed her cheeks. It was late afternoon; the sun was behind the hospital, sinking toward the Pacific. Lona's eyes fluttered open. White robes, white sheets, green walls. A few books, a few tapes. An array of medical equipment thoughtfully sealed behind a locked sheet of clear sprayon. A private room! Who was paying for that? The last time the government scientists had paid. But now?

From her window she could see the twisted, tormented, thorny shapes of the cacti in the rear garden. Frowning, she made out two figures moving between the rows of rigid plants. One, quite a tall man, wore a buff-colored hospital gown. His shoulders were unusually broad. His hands and face were bandaged. He's been in a fire, Lona thought. The poor man. Beside him was a shorter man in business clothes, lean, restless. The tall one was pointing out a cactus to the other. Telling him something, perhaps lecturing him on cactus botany. And now reaching out with a bandaged hand. Touching the long, sharp spines. Watch out! You'll hurt yourself! He's sticking his hand right on the spines! Turning to the little one now. Pointing. The little one shaking his head – no, he doesn't want to stick himself on the spines.

The big one must be a little crazy, Lona decided.

She watched as they came nearer her window. She saw the smaller man's pointed ears and beady gray eyes. She could see nothing of the bigger man's face at all. Only the tiniest of slits broke the white wall of his bandage. Lona's mind quickly supplied the details of his mutilation: the corrugated skin, the flesh runneled and puddled by the flames, the lips drawn aside in a fixed sneer. But they could fix that. Surely they could give him a new face here. He would be all right.

Lona felt a profound envy. Yes, this man had suffered pain,

57

but soon the doctors would repair all that. His pain was only on the outside. They'd send him away, tall and strong and once more handsome, back to his wife, back to his . . .

. . . children.

The door opened. A nurse entered, a human one, not a robot. Though she might just as well have been. The smile was blank, impersonal.

'So you're up, dear? Did you sleep well? Don't try to talk, just nod. That's so good! I've come to get you ready. We're going to fix your lungs up a bit. It won't be any trouble at all for you – you'll just close your eyes and when you wake up, you'll be breathing good as new!'

It was merely the truth, as usual.

When they brought her back to her room, it was morning, so Lona knew that they had worked her over for several hours and then stored her in the post-op room. Now she was swathed in bandages herself. They had opened her body, had given her new segments of lung, and had closed her again. She felt no pain, not yet. The throbbing would come later. Would there be a scar? Sometimes there were scars after surgery even now, though generally not. Lona saw a jagged red track running from the hollow of her throat down between her breasts. Please, no, no scar.

She had hoped to die on the operating table. It had seemed like her last chance. Now she would have to go home, alive, unaltered.

The tall man was walking in the garden again. This time he was alone. And now he was without his bandages. Though his back was to her, Lona saw the bare neck, the edge of jaw. Once more he was examining the cacti. What was it about those ugly plants that drew him so? Down on his knees now, prodding at the spines. Now standing up. Turning.

Oh, the poor man!

Lona stared in shock and wonder at his face. He was too far away for the details to be visible, but the wrongness of it was plain to her.

This must have been the way they fixed him up, she thought. After the fire. But why couldn't they have given him an ordinary face? Why did they do that to him?

She could not take her eyes away. The sight of those artificial features fascinated her. He sauntered toward the building, moving slowly, confidently. A powerful man. A man who could suffer and bear it. I feel so sorry for him. I wish I could do something to help him.

She told herself she was being silly. He had a family. He'd get along.

Twelve

Hell Hath No Fury

Burris got the bad news on his fifth day at the hospital.

He was in the garden, as usual. Aoudad came to him.

'There can't be any skin grafts. The doctors say no. You're full of crazy antibodies.'

'I knew that already.' Calmly.

'Even your own skin rejects your skin.'

'I scarcely blame it,' Burris said.

They walked past the saguaro. 'You could wear some kind of mask. It would be a little uncomfortable, but they do a good job these days. The mask practically breaths. Porous plastic, right over your head. You'd get used to it in a week.'

'I'll think about it,' Burris promised. He knelt beside a small barrel cactus. Convex rows of spines took a great-circle route toward the pole. Flower buds seemed to be forming. The small glowing label in the earth said *Echinocactus grusonii*. Burris read it aloud.

'These cacti fascinate you so much,' said Aoudad. 'Why? What do they have for you?'

'Beauty.'

'*These?* They're all thorns!'

'I love cacti. I wish I could live forever in a garden of cacti.' A fingertip touched a spine. 'Do you know, on Manipool they have almost nothing but thorny succulents? I wouldn't call them cacti, of course, but the general effect is the same. It's a dry world. Pluvial belts about the poles, then mounting dryness approaching the Equator. It rains about every billion years at the Equator and somewhat more frequently in the temperate zones.'

'Homesick?'

'Hardly. But I learned the beauty of thorns there.'

'Thorns? They stick you.'

'That's part of their beauty.'

'You sound like Chalk now,' Aoudad muttered. 'Pain is instructive, he says. Pain is gain. And thorns are beautiful. Give me a rose.'

'Rose bushes are thorny, too,' Burris remarked quietly.

Aoudad looked distressed. 'Tulips, then. Tulips!'

Burris said, 'The thorn is merely a highly evolved form of leaf. An adaptation to a harsh environment. Cacti can't afford to transpire the way leafy plants do. So they adapt. I'm sorry you regard such an elegant adaptation as ugly.'

'I guess I've never thought about it much. Look, Burris, Chalk would like you to stay here another week or two. There are some more tests.'

'But if facial surgery is impossible – '

'They want to check you out generally. With an eye toward the eventual body transplant.'

'I see.' Burris nodded briefly. He turned to the sun, letting the feeble winter beams strike his altered face. 'How good it is to stand in the sunlight again! I'm grateful to you, Bart, do you know that? You dragged me out of that room. That dark night of the soul. I feel everything thawing in me now, breaking loose, moving about. Am I mixing my metaphors? You see how less rigid I am already.'

'Are you flexible enough to entertain a visitor?'

'Who?' Instantly suspicious.

'Marco Prollisse's widow.'

'Elise? I thought she was in Rome!'

'Rome's an hour from here. She wants very badly to see you. She says you've been kept from her by the authorities. I won't force you, but I think you ought to let her see you. You could put the bandages on again, maybe.'

'No. No bandages, ever again. When will she be here?'

'She's already here. You just say the word and I'll produce her.'

'Bring her down, then. I'll see her in the garden. It's so much like Manipool here.'

Aoudad was strangely silent. At length he said, 'See her in your room.'

Burris shrugged. 'As you say.' He caressed the spines.

Nurses, orderlies, doctors, technicians, wheelchaired patients, all stared at him as he entered the building. Even two work-robots scanned him oddly, trying to match him against their programmed knowledge of human bodily configurations. Burris did not mind. His self-consciousness was eroding swiftly, day by day. The bandages he had worn on his first day here now seemed an absurd device. It was like going naked in public, he thought: first it seemed unthinkable, then, in time, it became tolerable, and at length customary. One had to accustom one's self.

Yet he was uneasy as he waited for Elise Prolisse.

He was at the window, watching the courtyard garden, when the knock came. Some last-minute impulse (tact or fear?) caused him to keep his back turned as she entered. The door closed timidly. He had not seen her in five years, but he remembered her as lush, somewhat overblown, a handsome woman. His enhanced hearing told him that she had come in alone, without Aoudad. Her breathing was ragged and hoarse. He heard her lock the door.

'Minner?' she said softly. 'Minner, turn around and look at me. It's all right. I can take it.'

This was different from showing himself to nameless hospital personnel. To his surprise, Burris found the seemingly solid serenity of the past few days dissolving swiftly. Panic clutched him. He longed to hide. But out of dismay came cruelty, an icy willingness to inflict pain. He pivoted on his heel and swung around to hurl his image into Elise Prolisse's large dark eyes.

Give her credit: she had resilience.

'Oh,' she whispered. 'Oh, Minner, it's' – a smooth shift of gears – 'not so awful. I heard it was much worse.'

'Do you think I'm handsome?'

'You don't frighten me. I thought it might be frightening.' She came toward him. She was wearing a clinging black tunic that probably had been sprayed on. High breasts were back in vogue, and that was where Elise wore hers, sprouting almost from her collar-bones, and deeply separated. Pectoral surgery was the secret. The deep mounds of flesh were wholly concealed by the tunic, and yet what kind of concealment could a micron of spray provide? Her hips flared; her thighs were pillars. But she had lost some weight. In the recent months of stress, no doubt, sleeplessness had shaved an inch or two from those continental buttocks. She was quite close to him now. Some dizzying perfume assailed him, and with no conscious effort at all Burris desensitized himself to it.

His hands slipped between hers.

61

His eyes met hers. When she flinched, it was only for the briefest instant.

'Did Marco die bravely?' she asked.

'He died like a man. Like the man he was.'

'Did you see?'

'Not the last moments, no. I saw them take him away. While we waited our turns.'

'You thought you would die, too?'

'I was sure of it. I said the last words for Malcondotto. He said them for me. But I came back.'

'Minner, Minner, Minner, how terrible it must have been!' She still clasped his hand. She was stroking the fingers . . . stroking even that tiny prehensile worm of flesh next to his littlest finger. Burris felt the wrench of amazement as she touched the loathsome thing. Her eyes were wide, solemn, tearless. She has two children, or is it three? But still young. Still vital. He wished she would release his hand. Her nearness was disturbing. He sensed radiations of warmth from her thighs, low enough on the electromagnetic spectrum, yet detectable. He would have bit his lips to choke back tension if his lips could fall between his teeth.

'When did you get the news about us?' he asked.

'When it came from the pickup station on Ganymede. They broke it to me very well. But I thought horrible things. I have to confess them to you. I wanted to know from God why it was that Marco had died and you had lived. I'm sorry, Minner.'

'Don't be. If I had my choice, I'd be the dead one and he'd be alive. Marco and Malcondotto both. Believe me. I'm not simply making words, Elise. I'd trade.'

He felt like a hypocrite. Better dead than mutilated, of course! But that was not the way she would understand his words. She'd see only the noble part, the unmarried survivor wishing he could lay down his life to spare the dead husbands and fathers. What could he tell her? He had sworn off whining.

'Tell me how it was,' she said, still holding his hand, tugging him down with her to sit on the edge of the bed. 'How they caught you. How they treated you. What it was like. I have to know!'

'An ordinary landing,' Burris told her. 'Standard landing and contact procedures. Not a bad world; dry; give it time and it'll be like Mars. Another two million years. Right now it's

62

Arizona shading into Sonora, with a good solid slash of Sahara. We met them. They met us.'

His eye-shutters clicked shut. He felt the blasting heat of the wind of Manipool. He saw the cactus shapes, snaky grayish plants twisting spikily along the sand for hundreds of yards. The vehicles of the natives came for him again.

'They were polite to us. They had been visited before, knew the whole contact routine. No space-flight themselves, but only because they weren't interested. They spoke a few languages. Malcondotto could talk with them. The gift of tongues; he spoke a Sirian dialect, and they followed. They were cordial, distant . . . alien. They took us away.'

A roof over his head with creatures growing in it. Not simple low-phylum things, either. No thermoluminescent fungi. These were backboned creatures sprouting from the arched roof.

Tubs of fermenting mash with other living things growing in them. Tiny pink bifurcated things with thrashing legs. Burris said, 'Strange place. But not hostile. They poked us a bit, prodded us. We talked. We carried out observations. After a while it dawned on us that we were in confinement.'

Elise's eyes were very glossy. They pursued his lips as the words tumbled from him.

'An advanced scientific culture, beyond doubt. Almost post-scientific. Certainly post-industrial. Malcondotto thought they were using fusion power, but we were never quite sure. After the third or fourth day we had no chance to check.'

She was not interested at all, he realized suddenly. She was barely listening. Then why had she come? Why had she asked? The story that was at the core of his being should be of concern to her, and yet there she stood, frowning, big-eyeing him, unlistening. He glowered at her. The door was locked. She cannot choose but hear. *And thus spake on that ancient man, the bright-eyed Mariner.*

'On the sixth day they came and took Marco away.'

A ripple of alertness. A fissure in that sleek surface of sensual blandness.

'We never saw him again alive. But we sensed that they were going to do something bad to him. Marco sensed it first. He always was a bit of a pre-cog.'

'Yes. Yes, he was. A little.'

'He left. Malcondotto and I speculated. Some days passed, and they came for Malcondotto, too. Marco hadn't returned.

63

Malcondotto talked with them before they took him. He learned that they had performed some sort of . . . experiment on Marco. A failure. They buried him without showing him to us. Then they went to work on Malcondotto.'

I've lost her again, he realized. She just doesn't care. A flicker of interest when I told her how Prolisse died. And then . . . *nulla.*

She cannot choose but hear.

'Days. They came for me. They showed me Malcondotto, dead. He looked . . . somewhat as I look now. Different. Worse. I couldn't understand what they were saying to me. A droning buzz, a chattering rasping sound. What sound would cacti make if they could talk? They put me back and let me stew awhile. I suppose they were reviewing their first two experiments, trying to see where they had gone wrong, which organs couldn't be fiddled with. I spent a million years waiting for them to come again. They came. They put me on a table, Elise. The rest you can see.'

'I love you,' she said.

'?'

'I want you, Minner. I'm burning.'

'It was a lonely trip home. They put me in my ship. I could still operate it, after a fashion. They rehabilitated me. I got going toward this system. The voyage was a bad one.'

'But you made it to Earth.'

How comes it, then, that thou art out of hell?

Why, this is hell, nor am I out of it.

He said, 'I made it, yes. I would have seen you when I landed, Elise, but you have to understand I wasn't a free agent. First they had me by the throat. Then they let go and I ran. You must forgive.'

'I forgive you. I love you.'

'Elise –'

She touched something at her throat. The polymerized chains of her garment gave up the ghost. Black shards of fabric lay at her ankles, and she stood bare before him.

So much flesh. Bursting with vitality. The heat of her was overpowering.

'Elise –'

'Come and touch me. With that strange body of yours. With those hands. I want to feel that curling thing you have on each hand. Stroking me.'

Her shoulders were wide. Her breasts were well anchored

64

by those strong piers and taut cables. The hips of the Earth-mother, the thighs of a courtesan. She was terribly close to him, and he shivered in the blaze, and then she stood back to let him see her in full.

'This isn't right, Elise.'

'But I love you! Don't you feel the force of it?'

'Yes. Yes.'

'You're all I have. Marco's gone. You saw him last. You're my link to him. And you're so – '

You are Helen, he thought.

' – beautiful.'

'Beautiful? I am beautiful?'

Chalk had said it, Duncan the Corpulent. *I daresay a lot of women would fling themselves at your feet . . . grotesqueness has its appeal.*

'Please, Elise, cover yourself.'

Now there was fury in the soft, warm eyes. 'You are not sick! You are strong enough!'

'Perhaps.'

'But you refuse me?' She pointed at his waist. 'These monsters – they did not destroy you. You are still a . . . man.'

'Perhaps.'

'Then – '

'I've been through so much, Elise.'

'And I have not?'

'You've lost your husband. That's as old as time, What's happened to me is brand-new. I don't want – '

'You are afraid?'

'No.'

'Then show me your body. Take away the robe. There is the bed!'

He hesitated. Surely she knew his guilty secret; he had coveted her for years. But one does not trifle with the wives of friends, and she was Marco's. Now Marco was dead. Elise glared at him, half melting with desire, half frigid with anger. Helen. She is Helen.

She flung herself against him.

The fleshy mounds quivering in intimate contact, the firm belly pressing close, the hands clutching at his shoulders. She was a tall woman. He saw the flash of her teeth. Then she was kissing him, devouring his mouth despite its rigidity.

Her lips suck forth my soul: see where it flies!

His hands were on the satiny smoothness of her back. His

nails indented the flesh. The little tentacles crawled in constricted circles. She forced him backward, toward the bed, the mantis-wife seizing her mate. *Come, Helen, come, give me my soul again.*

They toppled down together. Her black hair was pasted to her cheeks by sweat. Her breasts heaved wildly; her eyes had the gloss of jade. She clawed at his robe.

There are women who seek hunchbacks, women who seek amputees, women who seek the palsied, the lame, the decaying. Elise sought him. The hot tide of sensuality swept over him. His robe parted, and then he was bare to her.

He let her look upon him as he now was.

It was a test he prayed she would fail, but she did not fail it, for the full sight of him served only to stoke the furnace in her. He saw the flaring nostrils, the flushed skin. He was her captive, her victim.

She wins. But I will salvage something.

Turning to her, he seized her shoulders, forced her against the mattress, and covered her. This was her final triumph, woman-like, to lose in the moment of victory, to surrender at the last instant. Her thighs engulfed him. His too-smooth flesh embraced her silkiness. With a sudden great burst of demonic energy he mastered her and split her to the core.

Thirteen

Rosy-Fingered Dawn

Tom Nikolaides stepped into the room. The girl was awake now and looking out the window at the garden. He carried a small potted cactus, an ugly one, more gray than green and armed with vicious needles.

'Feeling better now, are you?'

'Yes,' Lona said. 'Much. Am I supposed to go home?'

'Not yet. Do you know who I am?'

'Not really.'

'Tom Nikolaides. Call me Nick. I'm in public relations. A response engineer.'

66

She received the information blankly. He put the cactus on the table beside her bed.

'I know all about you, Lona. In a small way I was connected with the baby experiment last year. Probably you've forgotten, but I interviewed you. I work for Duncan Chalk. Do you know who he is, perhaps?'

'Should I?'

'One of the richest men in the world. One of the most powerful. He owns newstapes . . . vidstations . . . He owns the Arcade. He takes a great interest in you.'

'Why did you bring me that plant?'

'Later. I – '

'It's very ugly.'

Nikolaides smiled. 'Lona, how would you like to have a couple of those babies that were born from your seed? Say, two of them, to raise as your own.'

'I don't think that's a very funny joke.'

Nikolaides watched the color spread over her hollow cheeks and saw the hard flame of desire come into her eyes. He felt like an unutterable bastard.

He said, 'Chalk can arrange it for you. You *are* their mother, you know. He could get a boy and a girl.'

'I don't believe you.'

Leaning forward, Nikolaides turned on the intense sincerity. 'You've got to believe me, Lona. You're an unhappy girl, I know. And I know *why* you're unhappy. Those babies. A hundred children pulled out of your body, taken away from you. And then they threw you aside, forgot you. As though you were just a thing, a robot baby-maker.'

She was interested now. But still skeptical.

He picked up the little cactus again and fondled the shiny pot, slipping his finger in and out of the drainage opening at the bottom. 'We can get you a couple of those babies,' he said to her open mouth, 'but not easily. Chalk would have to pull a lot of strings. He'll do it, but he wants you to do something for him in return.'

'If he's that rich, what could I do for him?'

'You could help another unhappy human being. As a personal favor to Mr Chalk. And then he'll help you.'

Her face was blank again.

Nikolaides leaned to her. 'There's a man right here in this hospital. Maybe you've seen him. Maybe you've heard about him. He's a starman. He went off to a strange planet and was

67

captured by monsters, and they messed him up. They took him apart and put him back together again the wrong way.'

'They did that to me,' Lona said, 'without even taking me apart first.'

'All right. He's been walking in the garden. A big man. From a distance perhaps you can't tell there's anything wrong with him, unless you can see his face. He has eyes that open like *this*. Sideways. And a mouth – I can't show you what the mouth does, but it isn't human. Close up, he's pretty scary. But he's still human inside, and he's a wonderful man, only naturally he's very angry over what they did to him. Chalk wants to help him. The way he wants to help him is by having someone be kind to him. You. You know what suffering is, Lona. Meet this man. Be good to him. Show him that he's still people, that someone can love him. Bring him back to himself. And if you do that, Chalk will see that you get your babies.'

'Am I supposed to sleep with him?'

'You're supposed to be kind to him. I don't expect to tell you what that means. Do whatever would make him happy. You'll be the judge. Just take your own feelings, turn them around, inside out. You'll know a little of what he's going through.'

'Because he's been made a freak. And I was made a freak too.'

Nikolaides saw no tactful way of meeting that statement. He simply acknowledged it.

He said, 'This man's name is Minner Burris. His room is right across the hall from yours. He happens to be very much interested in cactus, God knows why. I thought you might send him this cactus as a get-well present. It's a nice gesture. It could lead to bigger things. Yes?'

'What was the name?'

'Nikolaides.'

'Not yours. His.'

'Minner Burris. And look, you could send a note with it. Don't minitype it, write it out yourself. I'll dictate it, and you make any changes you like.' His mouth was dry. 'Here. Here's the stylus . . .'

68

Fourteen

Happily Ever After

With two of his closest aides off in the West performing a complex balletic *pas de quatre* with Burris and Lona, Duncan Chalk was forced to rely almost entirely on the services of Leontes d'Amore. D'Amore was capable, of course, or he'd never have come as far as he had. Yet he lacked Nikolaides's stability of character and also lacked Aoudad's consuming blend of ambition and insecurity. D'Amore was clever but shifty, a quicksand man.

Chalk was at home, in his lakeside palace. Tickers and newstapes chittered all about him, but he tuned them out with ease. D'Amore behind his left ear, Chalk patiently and speedily dealt with the towering stack of the daily business. The Emperor Ch'in Shih Huang Ti, so they said, had turned over a hundred and twenty pounds of documents a day and still had sufficient spare time to build the Great Wall. Of course, documents were written on bamboo slabs in those days, much heavier than minislips. But old Shih Huang Ti had to be admired. He was one of Chad's heroes.

He said, 'What time did Aoudad phone in that report?'

'An hour before you awoke.'

'I should have been awakened. You know that. He knows that.'

D'Amore's lips performed an elegant entrechat of distress. 'Since there was no crisis, we felt – '

'You were wrong.' Chalk pivoted and nailed d'Amore with a quick glance. D'Amore's discomfort fed Chalk's needs to some extent, but not sufficiently. The petty writhings of underlings were no more nourishing than straw. He needed red meat. He said, 'So Burris and the girl have been introduced.'

'Very successfully.'

'I wish I could have seen it. How did they take to each other?'

'They're both edgy. But basically sympathetic. Aoudad thinks it'll work out well.'

'Have you planned an itinerary for them yet?'

69

'It's coming along. Luna Tivoli, Titan, the whole interplanetary circuit. Though we'll start them in the Antarctic. Accommodations, details – everything's under control.'

'Good. A cosmic honeymoon. Maybe even a small bundle of joy to brighten the tale. That would be something, if he turned out fertile! We know *she* is, by God!'

D'Amore said worriedly, 'Concerning that: the Prolisse woman is undergoing tests even now.'

'So you've got her. Splendid, splendid! Did she resist?'

'She was given a valid cover story. She thinks she's being checked for alien viruses. By the time she wakes up, we'll have the semen analysis and our answer.'

Chalk nodded brusquely. D'Amore left him, and the large man scooped the tape of Elise's visit to Burris from its socket and fitted it into the viewer for another scanning. Chalk had been against the idea of letting her see him, at first, despite Aoudad's strong recommendation. But in short order Chalk had come to understand some advantages of it. Burris had not had a woman since his return to Earth. Signora Prolisse, according to Aoudad (who was in a position to know!) had a peppery hunger for the distorted body of her late husband's shipmate. Let them get together, then; see Burris's response. A prize bull should not be nudged into a highly publicized mating without some preliminary tests.

The tape was graphic and explicit. Three hidden cameras, only a few molecules in lens diameter, had recorded everything. Chalk had viewed the sequence three times, but there were always new subtleties to derive. Watching unsuspecting couples in the act of love gave him no particular thrill; he obtained his pleasures in more refined manners, and the sight of the beast with two backs was interesting only to adolescents. But it was useful to know something of Burris's performance.

He sped the tape past the preliminary conversation. How bored she seems while he tells of his adventures! How frightened he seems when she exposes her body! What terrifies him? He is no stranger to women. Of course, that was in his old life. Perhaps he fears that she will find his new body hideous and turn away from him at the crucial instant. The moment of truth. Chalk pondered it. The cameras could not reveal Burris's thoughts, nor even his emiotional constellation, but Chalk himself had not taken steps to detect his inner feelings. So all had to be by inference.

Certainly Burris was reluctant. Certainly the lady was determined. Chalk studied the naked tigress as she staked out her claim. It seemed for a while as though Burris would spurn her – not interested in sex, or in any event not interested in Elise. Too noble to top his friend's widow? Or still afraid to open himself to her, even in the face of her unquestioned yearning? Well, he was raked now. Elise still undeterred. The doctors who had examined Burris upon his return said that he was still capable of the act – so far as they could tell – and now it was quite clear that they had been right.

Elise's arms and legs waved aloft. Chalk tugged at his dew-laps as the tiny figures on the screen acted out the rite. Yes, Burris could make love even now. Chalk lost interest as the coupling ran to its climax. The tape petered out after a final shot of limp, depleted figures side by side on the rumpled bed. He could make love, but what about babies? Chalk's men had intercepted Elise soon after she had left Burris's room. A few hours ago the lusty wench had lain unconscious on a doctor's table, the heavy legs apart. But Chalk sensed that this time he was bound to be disappointed. Many things were within his control; not all.

D'Amore was back. 'The report's in.'

'And?'

'No fertile sperm. They can't quite figure out what they've got, but they swear it won't reproduce. The aliens must have done a switch there, too.'

'Too bad,' Chalk sighed. 'That's one line of approach we'll have to scratch. The future Mrs Burris won't have any children by him.'

D'Amore laughed. 'She's got enough babies already, hasn't she?'

Fifteen

The Marriage of True Minds

To Burris, the girl had little sensual appeal coming along as she did in the wake of Elise Prolisse. But he liked her. She was a kindly, pathetic, fragile child. She meant well. The potted

71

cactus touched him. It seemed too humble a gesture to be anything but friendliness.

And she was unappalled by his appearance. Moved, yes. A bit queasy, yes. But she looked him right in the eye, concealing any dismay she might feel.

He said, 'Are you from around here?'

'No. I'm from back East. Please sit down. Don't stand up on my account.'

'It's all right. I'm really quite strong, you know.'

'Are they going to do anything for you here in the hospital?'

'Just tests. They have an idea they can take me out of this body and put me into a normal human one.'

'How wonderful!'

'Don't tell anyone, but I suspect it isn't going to work. The whole thing's a million miles up right now, and before they bring it down to Earth – ' He spun the cactus on the bedside table. 'But why are you in the hospital, Lona?'

'They had to fix my lungs some. Also my nose and throat.'

'Hayfever?' he asked.

'I put my head in a disposal sac,' she said simply.

A crater yawned briefly beneath Burris's feet. He clung to his equilibrium. What rocked him, as much as what she had said, was the toneless way she had said it. As though it were nothing at all to let acid eat your bronchi.

'You tried to kill yourself?' he blurted.

'Yes. They found me fast, though.'

'But – why? At your age!' Patronizingly, hating himself for the tone. 'You have everything to live for!'

The eyes grew big. Yet they lacked depth; he could not help contrasting them with the smoldering coals in Elise's sockets. 'You don't know about me?' she asked, voice still small.

Burris grinned. 'I'm afraid not.'

'Lona Kelvin. Maybe you didn't catch the name. Or maybe you forgot. I know. You were still out in space when it all happened.'

'You've lost me two turns back.'

'I was in an experiment. Multiple-embryo ova-transplantation, they called it. They took a few hundred eggs out of me and fertilized them and grew them. Some in the bodies of other women, some in incubator things. About a hundred of the babies were born. It took six months. They experimented on me last year just about this time.'

The last ledge of false assumptions crumbled beneath him.

72

Burris had seen a high-school girl, polite, empty-headed, concerned to some mild extent about the strange creature in the room across the hall, but mainly involved with the tastes and fashions, whatever they were, of her chronological peer group. Perhaps she was here to have her appendix dissolved, or for a nose bob. Who could tell? But suddenly the ground had shifted and he started to view her in a more cosmic light. A victim of the universe.

'A hundred babies? I never heard a thing about it, Lona!'

'You must have been away. They made a big fuss.'

'*How* old are you?'

'Seventeen now.'

'You didn't bear any of the babies yourself, then?'

'No. No. That's the whole thing. They took the eggs away from me, and that was where it all stopped, for me. Of course, I got a lot of publicity. Too much.' She peered at him shyly. 'I'm boring you, all this talk about myself.'

'But I want to know.'

'It isn't very interesting. I was on the vid a lot. And in the tapes. They wouldn't leave me alone. I had nothing much to say, because I hadn't *done* anything, you know. Just a donor. But when my name got out, they came around to me. Reporters all the time. Never alone, and yet always alone, do you know? So I couldn't take it any more. All I wanted – a couple of babies out of my own body, not a hundred babies out of machines. So I tried to kill myself.'

'By putting your head in a disposal sac.'

'No, that was the second time. The first, I jumped under a truck.'

'When was that?' Burris asked.

'Last summer. They brought me here and fixed me up. Then they sent me back East again. I lived in a room. I was afraid of everything. It got too scary, and I found myself going down the hall to the dissolver room and opening the disposal sac and – well . . . I didn't make it again. I'm still alive.'

'Do you still want to die so badly, Lona?'

'I don't know.' The thin hands made clutching motions in mid-air. 'If I only had something to hang onto . . . But look, I'm not supposed to be talking about me. I just wanted you to know a little of why I was here. You're the one who – '

'Not *supposed* to be talking about yourself? Who says?'

Dots of color blazed in the sunken cheeks. 'Oh, I don't

know. I mean, I'm not really important. Let's talk about space, Colonel Burris!'

'Not Colonel. Minner.'

'Out there – '

'Are Things that catch you and change you all around. That's what space is, Lona.'

'How terrible!'

'I think so, too. But don't reinforce my convictions.'

'I don't follow.'

'I feel terribly sorry for myself,' Burris said. 'If you give me half a chance, I'll pour your shell-like ear full of bad news. I'll tell you just how unfair I think it was for them to have done this to me. I'll gabble about the injustice of the blind universe. I'll talk a lot of foolishness.'

'But you've got a *right* to be angry about it! You didn't mean any harm to them. They just took you and – '

'Yes.'

'It wasn't decent of them!'

'I know, Lona. But I've already said that at great length, mostly to myself but also to anyone who'd listen. It's practically the only thing I say or think. And so I've undergone a second transformation. From man to monster; from monster to walking embodiment of injustice.'

She looked puzzled. I'm talking over her head, he told himself.

He said, 'What I mean is, I've let this thing that happened to me *become* me. I'm a thing, a commodity, a moral event. Other men have ambitions, desires, accomplishments, attainments. I've got my mutilation, and it's devouring me. *Has* devoured me. So I try to escape from it.'

'You're saying that you'd rather not talk about what happened to you?' Lona asked.

'Something like that.'

She nodded. He saw her nostrils flicker, saw her thin lips curl in animation. A smile burst forth. 'You know, Col – Minner – it's a little bit the same way with me. I mean, being a victim and all, and feeling so sorry for yourself. They did something bad to me, too, and since then all I do is go back and think about it and get angry. Or sick. And the thing I really should be doing is forgetting about it and going on to something else.'

'Yes.'

'But I can't. Instead I keep trying to kill myself because I

74

decide I can't bear it.' Her eyes faltered to the floor. 'Do you mind if I ask – have you – have you ever tried – ?

A halt.

'To kill myself since this happened? No. No, Lona. I just brood. Slow suicide, it's called.'

'We ought to make a deal,' she said. 'Instead of me feeling sorry for me, and you for you, let me feel sorry for you, and you feel sorry for me. And we'll tell each other how terrible the world has been to the other one. But not to ourselves. I'm getting the words all mixed up, but do you know what I mean?'

'A mutual sympathy society. Victims of the universe, unite!' He laughed. 'Yes, I understand. Good idea, Lona! It's just what I – what we need. I mean, just what *you* need.'

'And what *you* need.'

She looked pleased with herself. She was smiling from fore-head to chin, and Burris was surprised at the change that came over her appearance when that glow of self-satisfaction ap-peared. She seemed to grow a year or two older, to pick up strength and poise. And even womanliness. For an instant she was no longer skinny and pathetic. But then the glow faded and she was a little girl again.

'Do you like to play card games?'

'Yes.'

'Can you play Ten Planets?'

'If you'll teach me,' Burris said.

'I'll go get the cards.'

She bounced out of the room, her robe fluttering around her slim figure. Returning a moment later with a deck of waxy-looking cards, she joined him on the bed. Burris's quick eyes were on her when the middle snap of her pajama top lost polarity, and he caught a glimpse of a small, taut white breast within. She brushed her hand over the snap an instant later. She was not quite a woman, Burris told himself, but not a child, either. And then he reminded himself: this slender girl is the mother (?) of a hundred babies.

'Have you ever played the game?' she asked.

'Afraid not.'

'It's quite simple. First I deal ten cards apiece – ?

Sixteen

The Owl, For All His Feathers, Was A-Cold

They stood together by the hospital power plant, looking through the transparent wall. Within, something fibrous lashed and churned as it picked up energy from the nearest pylon and fed it to the transformer bank. Burris was explaining to her about how power was transmitted that way, without wires. Lona tried to listen, but she did not really care enough about finding out. It was hard to concentrate on something like that, so remote from her experience. Especially with *him* beside her.

'Quite a contrast from the old days,' he was saying. 'I can still recall a time when the million-kv lines were strung across the countryside, and they were talking of stepping the voltage up to a million and a half – '

'You know so many things. How did you have time to learn all that about electricity if you had to be a starman, too?'

'I'm terribly old,' he said.

'I bet you aren't even eighty yet.'

She was joking, but he didn't seem to realize it. His face quirked in that funny way, the lips (were they still to be called lips?) pulling outward toward his cheeks. 'I'm forty years old,' he said hollowly. 'I suppose to you forty is most of the way to being eighty.'

'Not quite.'

'Let's go look at the garden.'

'All those sharp pointed things!'

'You don't like them,' he said.

'Oh, no, no, no,' Lona insisted, recovering quickly. He likes the cacti, she sold herself. I mustn't criticize the things he likes. He needs someone to like the things he likes. Even if they aren't very pretty.

They strolled toward the garden. It was noon, and the pale sun cut sharp shadows into the crisp, dry earth. Lona shivered. She had a coat on over her hospital gown, but even so, even here in the desert, it was a cold day. Burris, lightly dressed, didn't seem to mind the chill. Lona wondered whether that new body of his had some way of adjusting to meet the temperature, like a snake's. But she didn't ask. She tried not to talk to him about his body. And the more she thought about it, the more it seemed to her that a snake's way of adjusting to cold weather was to crawl off and go to sleep. She let the point pass.

He told her a great deal about cacti.

They paced the garden, up and down, through the avenues of bristling plants. Not a leaf, not even a bough. Nor a flower. Here are buds, though, he told her. This one will have a fine red apple-like fruit in June. They make candy from this one. Thorns and all? Oh, no, not the thorns. He laughed. She laughed, too. She wanted to reach out and take him by the hand. What would it be like, feeling that curling extra thing against her fingers?

She had expected to be afraid of him. It surprised her, but she felt no fear.

She wished he would take her inside, though.

He pointed to a blurred shape hovering over one of the nastiest-looking of the cactus plants. 'Look there!'

'A big moth?'

'Hummingbird, silly! He must be lost.' Burris moved forward, obviously excited. Lona saw the things on his hands wriggle around, as they often did when he wasn't paying attention to them. He was down on one knee, peering at the hummingbird. She looked at him in profile, observing the strong jaw, the flat drumhead of twanging skin where an ear should have been. Then, because he would want her to, she looked at the bird. She saw a tiny body and what could perhaps be a long, straight bill. A dark cloud hung about the bird. 'Are those its wings?' she asked.

'Yes. Beating terribly fast. You can't see them, can you?'

'Just a blur.'

'I see the individual wings. Lona, it's incredible! I see the wings! With these eyes!'

'That's wonderful, Minner.'

'The bird's a stray; probably belongs in Mexico, probably wishes he were there now. He'll die up here before he finds a flower. I wish I could do something.'

'Catch him? Have someone take him to Mexico?'

Burris looked at his hands as if weighing the possibility of seizing the hummingbird in a lightning swoop. Then he shook his head. 'My hands couldn't be fast enough, even now. Or I'd crush him if I caught him. I – there he goes!'

And there he went. Lona watched the brown blur vanish down the garden. At least he's going south, she thought. She turned to Burris.

'It pleases you some of the time, doesn't it?' she asked. 'You like it . . . a little.'

'Like what?'

'Your new body.'

He quivered a little. She wished she hadn't mentioned it.

He seemed to check a first rush of words. He said, 'It has a few advantages, I admit.'

'Minner, I'm cold.'

'Shall we go inside?'

'If you don't mind.'

'Anything you say, Lona.'

They moved side by side toward the door. Their shadows dribbled off to their left at a sharp angle. He was much taller than she was, nearly a foot. And very strong. I wish. That he would take me. In his arms.

She was not at all put off by his appearance.

Of course, she had seen only his head and his hands. He might have a huge staring eye set in the middle of his chest. Or a mouth under each arm. A tail. Big purple spots. But as the fantasies welled through her mind, it struck her that even those inventions were not really frightening. If she could get used to his face and his hands, as she had so speedily, what would further differences matter? He had no ears, his nose was not a nose, his eyes and his lips were strange, his tongue and his teeth were like something out of a dream. And each hand had that extra thing. Yet quite rapidly she had stopped noticing. His voice was pleasant and normal, and he was so smart, so interesting. And he seemed to like her. Was he married, she wondered. How could she ask?

The hospital door bellied inward as they approached.

'My room?' he asked. 'Or yours?'

'What will we do now?'

'Sit. Talk. Play cards.'

'Playing cards bored you.'

'Did I ever say it did?' he asked her.

'You were too polite. But I could tell. I could see you were hiding it. It was written all over your . . . ' Her voice trailed off. 'Face.'

It keeps coming back, she thought.

'Here's my room,' she said.

Which room they went to hardly mattered. They were identical, one facing the rear garden where they had just been, one facing the courtyard. A bed, a desk, an array of medical equipment. He took the bedside chair. She sat on the bed. She wanted him to come over and touch her body, warm her chilled flesh, but of course she did not dare suggest it.

'Minner, how soon will you be leaving the hospital?'

'Soon. A few days. What about you, Lona?'

'I guess I could go out almost any time now. What will you do when you leave?'

'I'm not sure. I think I'll travel. See the world, let the world see me.'

'I've always wanted to travel,' she said. Too obvious. 'I've never really been anywhere.'

'Such as where?'

'Luna Tivoli,' she said. 'Or the Crystal Planet. Or – well, anywhere. China. The Antarctic.'

'It's not hard to get there. You get on the liner and go.' For an instant his face sealed itself, and she did not know what to think; the lips slid shut, the eyes clicked their lids into place. She thought of a turtle. Then Burris opened again and said, astonishing her, 'What if we went to some of those places together?'

Seventeen

Take Up These Splinters

Somewhat higher than the atmosphere Chalk soared. He looked upon his world and found it good. The seas were green verging on blue, or blue verging on green, and it seemed to him that he could discern icebergs adrift. The land was brown in winter's grip, to the north; summer-green lay below the curving middle.

He spent much of his time in lower space. It was the best way, the most esthetically satisfying way, of shunning gravity. Perhaps his pilot felt distress, for Chalk did not permit the use of reverse gravitrons up here, nor even any centrifuging to provide the illusion of weight. But his pilot was paid well enough to endure such discomforts, if discomforts they were.

For Chalk it was not remotely a discomfort to be weightless. He had his mass, his wonderful brontosaurian mass, and yet he had none of the drawbacks thereof.

'This is one of the few instances,' he said to Burris and the girl, 'where one can legitimately get something for nothing. Consider: when we blast off, we dissipate the gravity of acceleration through gravitrons, so that the extra Gs are squirted away and we rise in comfort. There's no effort for us in getting where we are, no price to pay in extra weight before we can be weightless. When we land, we treat the deceleration problem the same way. Normal weight, weightless, normal again, and no flattening at any time.'

'But is it free?' Lona asked. 'I mean, it must cost a lot to run the gravitrons. When you balance everything out, the expense of starting and stopping, you haven't really had anything for nothing, have you?'

Chalk, amused, looked at Burris. 'She's very clever, did you realize that?'

'So I've been noticing.'

Lona reddened. 'You're making fun of me.'

'No, we aren't,' said Burris. 'You've hit quite independently on the notion of conservation of gravity, don't you see? But you're being too strict with our host. He's looking at things from his point of view. If he doesn't have to feel the buildup of Gs himself, it doesn't cost him anything in the realest sense of the word. Not in terms of enduring high G. The gravitrons absorb all that. Look, it's like committing a crime, Lona, and paying someone else to go through rehabilitation. Sure, it costs you cash to find a rehab substitute. But you've had your crime, and he takes the punishment. The cash equivalent – '

'Let it go,' Lona said. 'It's nice up here, anyway.'

'You like weightlessness?' Chalk asked. 'Have you ever experienced it before?'

'Not really. A few short trips.'

'And you, Burris? Does the lack of gravity help your discomforts any?'

'A little, thanks. There's no drag on the organs that aren't where they really ought to be. I don't feel that damned pulling in my chest. A small mercy, but I'm grateful.'

Nevertheless, Burris was still in his bath of pain, Chalk noticed. Perhaps more tepid, but not enough. What was it like to feel constant physical discomfort? Chalk knew a little of that, simply through the effort of hauling his body around in full gravity. But he had been bloated so long. He was accustomed to the steady aching pull. Borris, though? The sensations of nails being hammered into his flesh? He did not protest. Only now and then did the bitter rebellion surge to the surface. Burris was improving, learning to accommodate to what was for him the human condition. Chalk, sensitive as he was, still picked up the emanations of pain. Not merely psychic pain. Physical pain, too. Burris had grown calmer, had risen from the black pit of depression in which Aoudad had first encountered him, but he was far from any beds of roses.

The girl, comparatively, was in better shape, Chalk concluded. She was not quite so intricate a mechanism.

They looked happy side by side, Burris and the girl.

That would change, of course, as time went on.

'You see Hawaii?' Chalk asked. 'And there, by the edge of the world: China. The Great Wall. We've had it restored, a good deal of it. See, running inland from the sea just above that gulf. Passing north of Peking, up into those mountains. The middle section is gone, the Ordos desert stretch. But then it was never very much, just a line of mud. And beyond, toward Sinkiang, see it coming up now? We have several party centers along the Wall. A new one opening just on the Mongolian side shortly. Kublai Khan's Pleasure Dome.' Chalk laughed. 'But not stately. Anything but stately.'

They were holding hands, Chalk observed.

He concentrated on picking up their emotions. Nothing useful yet. From the girl came a kind of mild squashy contentment, a blank maternal sort of thing. Yes, she would. And from Burris? Not much of anything, so far. He was relaxed, more relaxed than Chalk had yet seen him to be. Burris liked the girl. She amused him, obviously. He enjoyed the attention she gave him. But he did not have any strong feeling toward her; he did not really think very much of her as a person. Soon she would be powerfully in love with him. Chalk thought it unlikely that the emotion would be reciprocated. Out of that difference in voltages an interesting current might be generated, Chalk surmised. A thermocouple effect, so to speak. We will see.

The ship hurtled westward over China, past the Kansu Panhandle, orbiting over the Old Silk Road.

Chalk said, 'I understand that you two will be leaving on

your travels tomorrow. So Nick tells me.'

'That's right. The itinerary's arranged,' said Burris.

'I can't wait. I'm so awfully excited!' Lona cried.

The schoolgirl blurt of words annoyed Burris. Chalk, well attuned to their shifting moods now, dug his receptors into the flash of irritation that rolled from him and gobbled it down. The burst of emotion was a sudden rent in a seamless velvet veil. A jagged dark streak across pearly gray smoothness. A beginning, Chalk thought. A beginning.

'It should be quite a trip,' he said. 'Billions of people wish you well.'

Eighteen

To the Toy Fair

You covered ground swiftly when you were in the hands of Duncan Chalk. Chalk's minions had conveyed them nonstop from the hospital to Chalk's private spaceport; then, after their flight around the world, they had been sped to the hotel. It was the most magnificent hotel the Western Hemisphere had ever known, a fact that seemed to dazzle Lona and that obscurely bothered Burris.

Entering the lobby, he slipped and began to fall.

That had been happening to him more and more, now that he was out in public. He had never really learned how to use his legs. His knees were elaborate ball-and-socket affairs, evidently designed to be frictionless, and at unpredictable moments they failed to support him. That was what happened now. There was a sensation as of his left leg disintegrating, and he began to slide toward the thick yellow carpet.

Vigilant robot bellhops sprang to his aid. Aoudad, whose reflexes were not quite as good as theirs, belatedly clutched at him. But Lona was closest. She flexed her knees and put her shoulder against his chest, supporting him while he clawed for balance. Burris was surprised at how strong she was. She held him up until the others reached him.

'Are you all right?' she asked breathlessly.

'More or less.' He swung his leg back and forth until he was sure the knee was locked in place again. Fiery pains shot as high as his hip. 'You were strong. You held me up.'

'It all happened so fast. I didn't know what I was doing. I just moved and there you were.'

'I'm so heavy, though.'

Aoudad had been holding him by the arm. As if slowly realizing it, he let go. 'Can you make it by yourself now?' he asked. 'What happened?'

'I forgot how my legs worked for a second,' Burris said. The pain was nearly blinding. He swallowed it down and, taking Lona's hand, slowly led the procession toward the gravitron bank. Nikolaides was taking care of the routine job of checking them in. They would be here two days. Aoudad entered the nearest liftshaft with them, and up they went.

'Eighty-two,' Aoudad said to the elevator's monitor-plate.

'Is it a big room?' Lona asked.

'It's a suite,' said Aoudad. 'It's lots of rooms.'

There were seven rooms altogether. A cluster of bedrooms, a kitchen, a lounging room, and a large conference room in which the representatives of the press would later gather. At Burris's quiet request, he and Lona had been given adjoining bedrooms. There was nothing physical between them yet. Burris knew that the longer he waited, the more difficult it would be, and yet he held back. He could not judge the depth of her feelings, and at this point he had grave doubts about his own.

Chalk had spared no expense to get them these accommodations. It was a lavish suite, hung with outworld draperies that throbbed and flickered with inner light. The spun-glass ornaments on the table, warmed in the hand, would sing sweet melodies. They were costly. The bed in his room was wide enough to hold a regiment. Hers was round and revolved at the touch of a switch. There were mirrors in the bedroom ceilings. At an adjustment, they contorted into diamond facets; at another, they became splintered shards; at another, they provided a steady reflection, larger and sharper than life. They could also be opaqued. Burris did not doubt that the rooms could play other tricks as well.

'Dinner tonight is in the Galactic Room,' Aoudad announced. 'You'll hold a press conference at eleven tomorrow morning. You meet with Chalk in the afternoon. The following morning you leave for the Pole.'

'Splendid.' Burris sat.

'Shall I have a doctor up to look at the leg?'

'It won't be necessary.'

'I'll be back in an hour and a half to escort you to dinner. You'll find clothes in the closets.'

Aoudad took his leave.

Lona's eyes were shining. She was in wonderland. Burris himself, not easily impressed by luxury, was at least interested in the extent of the comforts. He smiled at her. Her glow deepened. He winked.

'Let's look around again,' she murmured.

They toured the suite. Her room, his, the kitchen. She touched the program node of the food bank. 'We could eat here tonight,' he suggested. 'If you prefer, we can get everything we need.'

'Let's go out, though.'

'Of course.'

He did not need to shave, nor even to wash: small mercies of his new skin. But Lona was more nearly human. He left her in her room, staring at the vibraspray mounted in its cubicle. Its control panel was nearly as complex as that of a starship. Well, let her play with it.

He inspected his wardrobe.

They had stocked him as though he were going to be the star of a tridim drama. On one shelf were some twenty sprayon cans, each with its bright portrayal of its contents. In this one, green dinner jacket and lustrous purple-threaded tunic. In this, a single flowing robe decked with self-generating light. Here, a gaudy peacock thing with epaulets and jutting ribs. His own tastes ran to simpler designs, even to more conventional materials. Linen, cotton, the ancient fabrics. But his private tastes did not govern this enterprise. Left to his private tastes, he would be huddling in his flaking room in the Martlet Towers, talking to his own ghost. Here he was, a volunteer puppet dancing on Chalk's strings, and he had to dance the proper paces. This was his purgatory. He chose the epaulets and ribs.

Now, would the sprayon work?

His skin was strange in its porosity and other physical properties. It might reject the garment. Or – a waking nightmare – it might patiently undo the clinging molecules, so that in the twinkling of an eye his clothing shredded at the Galactic Room, leaving him not merely naked in a throng but exposed

84

in all his eerie otherness. He would chance it. Let them look. Let them see everything. The image crossed his mind of Elise Prolisse putting a hand to a secret stud and obliterating her black shroud in an instant, unveiling the white temptations. These clothes were unreliable. So be it. Burris stripped and inserted the sprayon can in the dispenser. He stepped beneath it.

Cunningly the garment shaped itself to his body.

The application took less than five minutes. Surveying his gaudiness in a mirror, Burris was not displeased. Lona would be proud of him.

He waited for her.

Nearly an hour went by. He heard nothing from her room. Surely she must be ready by now. 'Lona?' he called, and got no answer.

Panic speared him. This girl was suicide-prone. The pomp and elegance of this hotel might be just enough to tip her over the brink. They were a thousand feet above the ground here; she would not botch this attempt. I should never have left her alone, Burris told himself fiercely.

'*Lona!*'

He stepped through the widening partition into her room. Instantly he saw her and went numb with relief. She was in her closet, naked, her back to him. Narrow across the shoulders, narrower through the hips, so that the contrast of the narrow waist was lost. The spine rose like a subterranean burrow, steeply, shadowed. The buttocks were boyish. He regretted his intrusion. 'I didn't hear you,' he said. 'I was worried, and so when you didn't answer – '

She turned to him, and Burris saw that she had much more on her mind than her violated modesty. Her eyes were red-rimmed, her cheeks streaked. In a token of pudicity she lifted a thin arm across her small breasts, but the gesture was purely automatic and hid nothing. Her lips trembled. Beneath his outer skin he felt the shock of her body's impact, and he found himself wondering why so underfurnished a nudity should affect him this way. Because, he decided, it had lain beyond a barrier that now was shattered.

'Oh, Minner, Minner, I was ashamed to call you! I've been standing here for half an hour!'

'What's the trouble?'

'There's nothing for me to wear!'

He came closer. She turned aside, backing from the closet,

standing by his elbow and lowering the arm over her breasts. He peered into the closet. Dozens of sprayon cans were decked there. Fifty, a hundred of them.

'So?'

'I can't wear *those*!'

He picked one up. From the picture on the label it was a thing of night and fog, elegant, chaste, superb.

'Why can't you?'

'I want something simple. There's nothing simple here.'

'Simple? For the Galactic Room?'

'I'm afraid, Minner.'

And she was. The bare skin was goosebumped.

'You can be such a child sometimes!' he snapped.

The words fishhooked into her. She shrank back, looking more naked than ever, and fresh tears slipped from her eyes. The cruelty of the words seemed to linger in the room, like a silty deposit, after the words themselves were gone.

'If I'm a child,' she said hoarsely, 'why am I going to the Galactic Room?'

Take her in your arms? Comfort her? Burris was caught in wild eddies of uncertainty. He geared his voice for something that lay midway between parental anger and phony solicitousness and said, 'Don't be foolish, Lona. You're an important person. The whole world is going to look at you tonight and say how beautiful, how lucky you are. Put on something Cleopatra would have loved. And then tell yourself you're Cleopatra.'

'Do I look like Cleopatra?'

His eyes traveled her body. That was, he sensed, exactly what she wanted them to do. And he had to concede that she was less than voluptuous. Which perhaps she also sought to engineer from him. Yet, in her slight way, she was attractive. Even womanly. She shuttled between impish girlhood and neurotic womanhood.

'Pick one of these and put it on,' he said. 'You'll blossom to match. Don't be uneasy about it. Here I am in this insane costume, and I think it's wildly funny. You've got to match me. Go ahead.'

'That's the other trouble. There are so many. I can't pick!'

She had a point there. Burris stared into the closet. The choice was overwhelming. Cleopatra herself would have been dizzied, and this poor waif was stunned. He fished about uncomfortably, hoping to land on something that would instantly proclaim its suitability for Lona. But none of these garments had been designed for waifs, and so long as he persisted in thinking of her as one, he could make no selection. At last he came back to the one he had grabbed at random, the elegant and chaste one. 'This,' he said. 'I think this is just right.'

She looked doubtfully at the label. 'I'd feel embarrassed in anything so fancy.'

'We've dealt with that theme already, Lona. Put it on.'

'I can't use the machine. I don't know how.'

'It's the simplest thing in the world!' he burst out, and cursed himself for the ease with which he slipped into hectoring inflections with her. 'The instructions are right on the can. You put the can in the slot – '

'Do it for me.'

He did it for her. She stood in the dispenser zone, slim and pale and naked, while the garment issued forth in a fine mist and wrapped itself about her. Burris began to suspect that he had been manipulated, and rather adroitly at that. In one giant bound they had crossed the barrier of nudity, and now she showed herself to him as casually as though she were his wife of decades. Seeking his advice on clothing. Forcing him to stand by while she pirouetted beneath the dispenser, cloaking herself in elegance. The little witch! He admired the technique. The tears, the huddled bare body, the poor-little-girl approach. Or was he reading into her panic far more than was to be found there. Perhaps. Probably.

'How do I look?' she asked, stepping forth.

'Magnificent.' He meant it. 'There's the mirror. Decide for yourself.'

Her glow of pleasure was worth several kilowatts. Burris decided he had been all wrong about her motives; she was less complicated than that, had been genuinely terrified by the prospect of elegance, now was genuinely delighted at the ultimate effect.

Which was superb. The dispenser nozzle had spawned a gown that was not quite diaphanous, not quite skin-tight. It clung to her like a cloud, veiling the slender things and sloping shoulders and artfully managing to suggest a voluptuousness that was not there at all. No one wore undergarments with a sprayon outfit, and so the bare body lay just fractionally out of sight; but the designers were cunning, and the loose drape of this gown enhanced and amplified its wearer. The colors, too, were delicious. Through some molecular magic the polymers

87

were not tied strongly to one segment of the spectrum. As Lona moved the gown changed hue readily, sliding from dawn-gray to the blue of a summer sky, and thence to black, iron-brown, pearl, mauve.

Lona took on the semblance of sophistication that the garment provided her. She seemed taller, older, more alert, surer of herself. She held her shoulders up, and her breasts thrust forward in surprising transfiguration.

'Do you like it?' she asked softly.

'It's wonderful, Lona.'

'I feel so strange in it. I've never worn anything like this. Suddenly I'm Cinderella going to the ball!'

'With Duncan Chalk as your fairy godmother?'

They laughed. 'I hope he turns into a pumpkin at midnight,' she said. She moved toward the mirror. 'Minner, I'll be ready in another five minutes, all right?'

He returned to his own room. She needed not five minutes but fifteen to cleanse the evidence of tears from her face, but he forgave her. When she finally appeared, he scarcely recognized her. She had prettied her face to a burnished glamour that virtually transformed her. The eyes were rimmed now with shining dust; the lips gleamed in lush phosphorescence; earclips of gold covered her ears. She drifted like a wisp of morning mist into his room. 'We can go now,' she said throatily.

Burris was pleased and amused. In one sense, she was a little girl dressed up to look like a woman. In another, she was a woman just beginning to discover that she was no longer a girl. Had the chrysalis really opened yet? In any case he enjoyed the sight of her this way. She was certainly lovely. Perhaps fewer people would look at him, more at her.

They headed for the dropshaft together.

Just before he left his room, he notified Aoudad that he and Lona were coming down for dinner. Then they descended. Burris felt a wild surge of fear and grimly quelled it. This would be his most public exposure since his return to Earth. Dinner at the restaurant of restaurants; his strange face perhaps souring the caviar of a thousand fellow diners; eyes turned to him from all sides. He looked at it as a test. Somehow he drew strength from Lona and put on a cloak of courage as she had put on her unfamiliar finery.

When they reached the lobby, Burris heard the quick sighs of the onlookers. Pleasure? Awe? The *frisson* of delighted revulsion? He could not read their motives from their hissing uptake of air. Yet they were looking, and responding, to the strange pair who had emerged from the dropshaft.

Burris, Lona on his arm, kept his face taut. Get a good look at us, he thought sharply. The couple of the century, we are. The mutilated starman and the hundred-baby virgin mother. The show of the epoch.

They were looking, all right. Burris felt the eyetracks crossing his earless jaw, passing over his click-click eyelids and his rearranged mouth. He astounded himself by his own lack of response to their vulgar curiosity. They were looking at Lona, too, but she had less to offer them, since her scars were inward ones.

Suddenly there was commotion to Burris's left.

An instant later Elise Prolisse burst from the crowd and hurtled toward him, crying harshly, 'Minner! Minner!'

She looked like a she-berserker. Her face was bizarrely painted in a wild and monstrous parody of adornment: blue cheekstripes, red flanges over her eyes. She had shunned sprayon and wore a gown of some rustling, seductive natural fabric, cut low to reveal the milk-white globes of her breasts. Hands tipped with shining claws were outstretched.

'I've tried to get to you,' she panted. 'They wouldn't let me near you. They – '

Aoudad cut toward them. *'Elise – '*

She slashed his cheek with her nails. Aoudad reeled back, cursing, and Elise turned to Burris. She looked venom at Lona. She tugged at Burris's arm and said, 'Come away with me. Now that I've found you again I won't let go.'

'Get your hand off him!' From Lona. The syllables tipped with whirling blades.

The older woman glared at the girl. Burris, baffled, thought they would fight. Elise weighed at least forty pounds more than Lona, and, as Burris had good reason to know, she was fiercely strong. But Lona had unsuspected strengths, too.

A scene in the lobby, he thought with curious clarity. Nothing will be spared us.

'I love him, you little bitch!' Elise cried hoarsely.

Lona did not answer. But her hand moved out in a quick chopping gesture toward Elise's outstretched arm. Edge of hand collided with fleshy forearm in a quick crack. Elise hissed. She pulled back her arm. The hands formed claws again. Lona, squaring away, flexed her knees and was ready to leap.

All this had taken only seconds. Now the startled bystanders moved. Burris himself, after early paralysis, stepped in the way and shielded Lona from Elise's fury. Aoudad seized one of Elise's arms. She tried to pull it free, and her bare breasts quivered in the effort. Nikolaides moved in on the other side. Elise screamed, kicked, pulled, A circle of robot bellhops had formed. Burris watched as they dragged Elise away.

Lona leaned against an onyx pillar. Her face was deeply flushed, but otherwise not even her makeup was disarranged. She looked more startled than frightened.

'Who was that?' she asked.

'Elise Prolisse. The widow of one of my shipmates.'

'What did she want?'

'Who knows?' Burris lied.

Lona was not fooled. 'She said she loved you.'

'It's her privilege. I guess she's been under great stress.'

'I saw her in the hospital. She visited you.' Green flames of jealousy flickered across Lona's face. 'What does she want from you? Why did she make that scene?'

Aoudad came to his rescue. Holding a cloth to his bloodied cheek, he said, 'We've given her a sedative. She won't bother you again. I'm terribly sorry about this. A silly, hysterical fool of a woman – '

'Let's go back upstairs,' said Lona. 'I don't feel like eating in the Galactic Room now.'

'Oh, no,' Aoudad said. 'Don't cancel out. I'll give you a relaxer and you'll feel better in no time. You mustn't let a stupid episode like that spoil a wonderful evening.'

'At least let's get out of the lobby,' Burris said shortly.

The little group hurried toward a brightly lit inner room. Lona sank to a divan. Burris, crackling now with delayed tension, felt pain shoot through his thighs, his wrists, his chest. Aoudad produced a pocket tray of relaxers, taking one himself and giving one to Lona. Burris shrugged the little tube away, knowing that the drug it contained would have no effect on him. In moments Lona was smiling again.

He knew he had not been mistaken about the jealousy in her eyes. Elise had come up like a typhoon of flesh, threatening to sweep away all that Lona possessed, and Lona had fought back fiercely. Burris was both flattered and troubled. He could not deny that he enjoyed, as any man would, being the object of such a struggle. Yet that instant of revelation had shown him just how deeply Lona already was enmeshed with him. He felt no such depth of involvement himself. He liked the girl, yes, and was grateful to her for her company, but he was a long way from being in love with her. He doubted very much that he would ever love her, or anyone else. But she, without even the virtue of a physical bond linking them, had evidently constructed some inner fantasy of romance. The seeds of trouble lay in that, Burris knew.

Drained of tensions by Aoudad's relaxer, Lona quickly recovered from Elise's attack. They rose, Aoudad beaming again despite his injury.

'Will you go to dinner now?' he asked.

'I'm feeling much better,' Lona said. 'It was all so sudden – it shook me up.'

'Five minutes in the Galactic Room and you'll have forgotten the whole thing,' said Burris. He gave her his arm again. Aoudad conducted them toward the special liftshaft that led only to the Galactic Room. They mounted the gravity plate and sped upward. The restaurant was at the summit of the hotel, looking outward toward the heavens from its lofty spot like some private observatory, a sybaritic Uraniborg of food. Still trembling from the unexpected onslaught of Elise, Burris felt new anxiety as they reached the vestibule of the restaurant. He kept a calm front, but would he panic in the supernal glamour of the Galactic Room?

He had been there once before, long ago. But that was in another body, and besides, the wench was dead.

The liftshaft halted, and they stepped out into a bath of living light.

Aoudad said portentously, 'The Galactic Room! Your table is waiting. Enjoy yourselves.'

He vanished. Burris smiled tensely at Lona, who looked drugged and dazed with happiness and terror. The crystal doors opened for them. They went within.

Nineteen

Le Jardin Des Supplices

There had never been such a restaurant this side of Babylon.
Tier upon tier of terraces rose toward the starry dome. Refraction was banished here, and the dining-room seemed to be
open to the heavens, but in fact the elegant diners were shielded
from the elements at all times. A screen of black light framing
the façade of the hotel cancelled out the effect of the city
illumination, so that the stars always gleamed over the Galactic
Room as they would above an untenanted forest.

The far worlds of the universe thus lay only a short distance
out of reach. The things of those worlds, the harvest of the
stars, gave splendor to the room. The texture of its curving
walls was due to an array of alien artifacts: bright-hued
pebbles, Potsherds, paintings, tinkling magic-trees of odd
alloys, zigzagging constructions of living light, each embedded
in its proper niche in the procession of tiers. The tables seemed
to grow from the floor, which was carpeted with a not-quite-
sentient organism found on one of the worlds of Aldebaran.
The carpet was, to be blunt about it, not too different in structure and function from a Terran slime mold, but the management did not make too much ceremony over identifying it, and
the effect it produced was one of extreme richness.

Other things grew in select spots of the Galactic Room:
potted shrubs, sweet-smelling blossoming plants, even dwarf
trees, all (so it was said) imported from other worlds. The
chandelier itself was the product of alien hands: a colossal
efflorescence of golden tear-drops, crafted from the amber-like
secretion of a bulky sea-beast living along the gray shores of a
Centaurine planet.

It cost an incalculable sum to have dinner at the Galactic
Room. Every table was occupied, every night. One made
reservations weeks in advance. Those who had been lucky
enough to choose this night were granted the unexpected treat
of seeing the starman and the girl who had had the many
babies, but the diners, most of them celebrities themselves, had
only fleeting interest in the much-publicized pair. A quick look,

and then back to the wonders on one's plate.

Lona clung tightly to Burris's arm as they passed between the thick, clear doors. Her small fingers dug so deeply that she knew she must be hurting him. She found herself standing on a narrow raised platform looking out onto an enormous expanse of emptiness, with the starry sky blazing overhead. The core of the restaurant-dome was hollow and many hundreds of feet across; the tiers of tables clung like scales to the outer shell, giving every diner a window seat.

She felt as though she were tipping forward, tumbling into the ocean well before her.

'Oh!' Sharply. Knees trembling, throat dry, she rocked on her heels and quickly closed and opened her eyes. Terror pierced her in a thousand places. She might fall and be lost in the abyss; or her sprayon gown might deliquesce and leave her naked before this fashionable horde; or that she-witch with the giant udders might reappear and attack them as they ate; or she might commit some horrible blunder at the table; or, suddenly and violently ill, she might spray the carpet with her vomit. Anything might happen. This restaurant had been conceived in a dream, but not necessarily a good dream.

A furry voice out of nowhere murmured, 'Mr Burris, Miss Kelvin, welcome to the Galactic Room. Please step forward.'

'We get on that gravity plate,' Burris prompted her.

The coppery plate was a disk an inch thick and two yards in diameter, protruding from the rim of their platform. Burris led her onto it, and at once it slipped free of its mooring and glided outward and upward. Lona did not look down. The floating plate took them to the far side of the great room and came to rest beside a vacant table perched precariously on a cantilevered ledge. Dismounting, Burris helped Lona to the ledge. Their carrier disk fluttered away, returning to its place. Lona saw it edge-on for a moment, wearing a gaudy corona of reflected light.

The table, on a single leg, appeared to sprout organically from the ledge. Lona gratefully planted herself on her chair, which molded itself instantly to the contours of her back and buttocks. There was something obscene about that confident grip, and yet it was reassuring; the chair, she thought, would not release her if she became dizzy and started to slide toward the steep drop to her left.

'How do you like it?' Burris asked, looking into her eyes.

'It's incredible. I never imagined it was like this.' She did not tell him that she was nearly sick from the impact of it.

'We have a choice table. It's probably the one Chalk himself uses when he eats here.'

'I never knew there were so many stars!'

They looked up. From where they sat they had an unimpeded view of almost a hundred and fifty degrees of arc. Burris told her the stars and planets.

'Mars,' he said. 'That's easy: the big orange one. But can you see Saturn? The rings aren't visible, of course, but . . . ' He took her hand, aimed it, and described the lay of the heavens until she thought she saw what he meant. 'We'll be out there soon, Lona. Titan's not visible from here, not with naked eye, but we'll be on it ourselves before long. And then we'll see those rings! Look, look there: Orion. And Pegasus.' He called off the constellations for her. He named stars with a sensuous pleasure in uttering the sounds of them: Sirius, Arcturus, Polaris, Bellatrix, Rigel, Algol, Antares, Betelgeuse, Aldebaran, Procyon, Markab, Deneb, Vega, Alphecca. 'Each of them a sun,' he said. 'Most have worlds. And there they all are spread out before us!'

'Have you visited many other suns?'

'Eleven. Nine with planets.'

'Including any of the ones you just named? I like those names.'

He shook his head. 'The suns I went to had numbers, not names. At least, not names Earthmen had given. Most of them had other names. Some I learned.' She saw the corners of his mouth pulling open and rapidly drawing closed again: a sign of tension in him, Lona had learned. *Should I talk about the stars to him? Perhaps he doesn't want to be reminded.*

Under this bright canopy, though, she could not leave the theme alone.

'Will you ever go back out there?' she asked.

'Out of this system? I doubt it. I'm retired from the service now. And we don't have tourist flights to neighboring stars. But I'll be off Earth again, of course. With you: the planetary tour. Not quite the same. But safer.'

'Can you – can you – ' she debated and rushed onward – 'show me the planet where you were – captured?'

Three quick contortions of his mouth. 'It's a bluish sun. You can't see it from this hemisphere. You can't see it with naked eye even down below. Six planets. Manipool's the fourth. When we were orbiting it, coming around ready to go down, I felt a strange excitement. As though my destiny drew me to this place. Maybe there's a little tinge of the pre-cog in me, eh, Lona? Surely Manipool had its large place in my destiny. But I can tell I'm no pre-cog. From time to time I'm hit with this powerful conviction that I'm marked for a return trip. And that's absurd. To go back *there* . . . to confront Them again . . .' His fist closed suddenly, tightening with a convulsive snap that pulled his entire arm inward. A vase of thick-petaled blue flowers nearly went flying into the void. Lona caught it. She noticed that when he closed his hand, the little outer tentacle neatly wrapped itself across the backs of his fingers. Putting both of her hands over his, she held him by the knuckles until the tension ebbed and his fingers opened.

'Let's not talk of Manipool,' she suggested. 'The stars are beautiful, though.'

'Yes. I never really thought of them that way until I came back to Earth after my first voyage. We see them only as dots of light, from down here. But when you're out there caught in the crisscross of starlight, bouncing this way and that as the stars buffet you, it's different. They leave a mark on you. Do you know, Lona, that you get a view of the stars from this room that's almost as piercing as what you see from the port of a starship?'

'How do they do it? I've never seen anything like that.'

He tried to explain about the curtain of black light. Lona was lost after the third sentence, but she stared intently into his strange eyes, pretending to listen and knowing that she must not be deceiving him. He knew so much! And yet he was frightened in this room of delights, just as she was frightened. So long as they kept talking, it created a barrier against the fear. But in the silences Lona was awkwardly aware of the hundreds of rich, sophisticated people all about her, and of the overwhelming luxury of the room, and of the abyss beside her, and of her own ignorance and inexperience. She felt naked beneath that blaze of stars. In the interstices of the conversation even Burris again became strange to her; his surgical distortions, which she had nearly ceased to notice, abruptly took on a fiery conspicuousness.

'Something to drink?' he asked.

'Yes. Yes, please. You order. I don't know what to have.'

No waiter, human or robot, was in sight, nor did Lona see any attending at the other tables. Burris gave the order simply by uttering it into a golden grillwork at his left elbow. His cool knowledgeableness awed her, as she half suspected it was meant to do. She said. 'Have you eaten here often? You seem to know what to do.'

'I was here once. More than a decade ago. It's not a place you forget easily.'

'Were you a starman already, then?'

'Oh, yes. I'd made a couple of trips. I was on furlough. There was this girl I wanted to impress – '

'Oh.'

'I didn't impress her. She married someone else. They were killed when the Wheel collapsed, on their honeymoon,'

Ten years and more ago, Lona thought. She had been less than seven years old. She felt shriveled with her youthfulness beside him. She was glad when the drinks arrived.

They came skimming across the abyss on a small gravitation tray. It seemed amazing to Lona that none of the serving trays, which now she noticed were quite numerous, ever collided as they soared to their tables. But, of course, it was no great task to program non-intersecting orbits.

Her drink came in a bowl of polished black stone, thick to the hand but smooth and gracile to the lip. She scooped up the bowl and automatically took it toward her mouth; then, halting an instant before the sip, she realized her error. Burris waited, smiling, his own glass still before him.

He seems so damned schoolmasterish when he smiles like that, she thought. Scolding me without saying a word. I know what he's thinking: that I'm an ignorant little tramp who doesn't know her manners.

She let the anger subside. It was really anger directed at herself, not him, she realized after a moment. Sensing that made it easier to grow calm.

She looked at his drink.

There was something swimming in it.

The glass was translucent quartz. It was three-fifths filled with a richly viscous green fluid. Moving idly back and forth was a tiny animal, teardrop-shaped, whose violet skin left a faint glow behind as it swam?

'Is that supposed to be there?'

Burris laughed. 'I have a Deneb martini, so-called. It's a preposterous name. Specialty of the house.'

'And in it?'

'A tadpole, essentially. Amphibious life-form from one of the Aldebaran worlds.'

'Which you drink?'

'Yes. Live.'

'Live.' Lona shuddered. 'Why? Does it taste that good?'

'It has no taste at all, as a matter of fact. It's pure decoration. Sophistication come full circle, back to barbarism. One gulp, and down it goes.'

'But it's alive! How can you kill it?'

'Have you ever eaten an oyster, Lona?'

'No. What's an oyster?'

'A mollusk. Once quite popular, served in its shell. Live. You sprinkle it with lemon juice – citric acid, you know – and it writhes. Then you seat it. It tastes of the sea. I'm sorry, Lona. That's how it is. Oysters don't know what's happening to them. They don't have hopes and fears and dreams. Neither does this creature here.'

'But to kill – '

'We kill to eat. A true morality of food would allow us to eat only synthetics.' Burris smiled kindly. 'I'm sorry. I wouldn't have ordered it if I'd known it would offend you. Shall I have them take it away?'

'No. Someone else would drink it, I guess. I didn't mean to say all that. I was just a little upset, Minner. But it's your drink. Enjoy it.'

'I'll send it back.'

'Please.' She touched the left-hand tentacle. 'You know why I object? Because it's like making yourself a god, to swallow a live living thing. I mean, here you are, gigantic, and you just destroy something, and it never knows why. The way – ' She stopped.

'The way alien Things can pick up an inferior organism and put it through surgery, without troubling to explain themselves?' he asked. 'The way doctors can perform an intricate experiment on a girl's ovaries, without considering later psychological effects? God, Lona, we've got to sidestep those thoughts, not keep coming back to them!'

'What did you order for me?' she asked.

'Gaudax. An aperitif from a Centaurine world. It's mild and sweet. You'll like it. Cheers, Lona.'

'Cheers.'

He moved his glass in orbit around her black stone bowl, saluting it and her. Then they drank. The Centaurine aperitif tickled her tongue; it was faintly oily stuff, yet delicate, delightful. She shivered with the pleasure. After three quick sips she put the bowl down.

The small swimming creature was gone from Burris's glass.

'Would you like to taste mine?' he asked.

'Please. No.'

He nodded. 'Let's order dinner, then. Will you forgive me for my thoughtlessness?'

Two dark green cubes, four inches on each face, sat side by side in the middle of the table. Lona had thought they were purely ornamental, but now, as Burris nudged one toward her, she realized that they were menus. As she handled it, warm light flushed through the depths of the cube and illuminated letters appeared, seemingly an inch below the sleek surface. She turned the cube over and over. Soups, meats, appetizers, sweets . . .

She recognized nothing on the menu.

'I shouldn't be in here, Minner. I just eat ordinary things. This is so weird I don't know where to begin.'

'Shall I order for you?'

'You'd better. Except they won't have the things I really want. Like a chopped protein steak and a glass of milk.'

'Forget the chopped protein steak. Sample some of the rarer delicacies.'

'It's so false, though. Me pretending to be a gourmet.'

'Don't pretend anything. Eat and enjoy. Chopped protein steak isn't the only food in the universe.'

His calmness reached forth to her, containing but not quite transferring to her. He ordered for both of them. Lona was proud of his skill. It was a small thing, knowing your way around a menu in such a place; yet he knew so much. He was awesome. She found herself thinking, *if only I had met him before they* . . . and cut the thought off. No imaginable set of circumstances would have brought her into contact with the premutilated Minner Burris. He would not have noticed her; he must have been busy then with women like that jiggly old Elise. Who still coveted him, but now could not have him. He's mine, Lona thought fiercely. He's mine! They tossed me a broken thing, and I'm helping to fix it, and no one will take it from me.

'Would you care for soup as well as an appetizer?' he asked.

'I'm not really terribly hungry.'

'Try a little anyway.'

'I'd only waste it.'

'No one worries about waste here. And we're not paying for this. Try.'

Dishes began to appear. Each was a specialty of some distant world, either imported authentically or else duplicated here with the greatest of craft. Swiftly the table was filled with strangeness. Plates, bowls, cups of oddities, served in stunning opulence. Burris called off the names to her and tried to explain the foods to her, but she was dizzied now and scarcely able to comprehend. What was this flaky white meat? These golden berries steeped in honey? This soup, pale and sprinkled with aromatic cheese? Earth alone produced so many cuisines; to have a galaxy to choose from was so dazzling a thought that it numbed the appetite.

Lona nibbled. She grew confused. A bite of this, a sip of that. She kept expecting the next goblet to contain some other little living creature. Long before the main course had arrived, she was full. Two kinds of wine had been brought. Burris mixed them and they changed color, turquoise and ruby blending to form an unexpected opal shade. 'Catalytic response,' he said. 'They calculate the esthetics of sight as well as of taste. Here.' But she could drink only a tiny bit.

Were the stars moving in ragged circles now?

She heard the hum of conversation all about her. For more than an hour she had been able to pretend that she and Burris had been isolated within a pocket of privacy, but now the presence of the other diners was breaking through. They were looking. Commenting. Moving about, drifting from table to table on their gravitron plates. Have you seen? What do you think of? How charming! How strange! How grotesque!

'Minner, let's get out of here.'

'But we haven't had our dessert yet.'

'I know. I don't care.'

'Liqueur from the Procyon group. Coffee Galactique.'

'Minner, no.' She saw his eyes open to the full shutter-width and knew that some expression on her face must have scored him deeply. She was very close to getting ill. Perhaps it was obvious to him.

'We'll go,' he told her. 'We'll come back for dessert some other time.'

'I'm so sorry, Minner,' she murmured. 'I didn't want to spoil the dinner. But this place . . . I just don't feel right in a place like this. It scares me. All these strange foods. The staring eyes. They're all looking at us, aren't they? If we could go

99

back to the room, it would be so much better.'

He was summoning the carrier disk now. Her chair released her from its intimate grip. Her legs were wobbly when she stood up. She did not know how she could take a step without toppling. A strange tunnel-like clarity of vision brought her isolated views as she hesitated. The fat jeweled woman with a host of chins. The gilded girl clad in transparency, not much older than herself but infinitely surer of herself. The garden of little forked trees two levels below. The ropes of living light festooned in the air. A tray slicing across the open space bearing three mugs of dark, shining unknownness. Lona swayed. Burris anchored her and virtually lifted her onto the disk, though to a watcher it would not seem that he held her in so supportive a way.

She stared fixedly forward as they crossed the gulf to the entrance platform.

Her face was flushed and beaded with sweat. Within her stomach, it seemed to her, the alien creatures had come to life and were swimming patiently in the digestive sauces. Somehow she and Burris passed through the crystal doors. Down to the lobby via quick dropshaft; then up again, another shaft, to their suite. She caught sight of Aoudad lurking in the corridor, disappearing quickly behind a broad pilaster.

Burris palmed the door. It opened for them.

'Are you sick?' he asked.

'I don't know. I'm glad to be out of there. It's so much calmer here. Did you lock the door?'

'Of course. Can I do anything for you, Lona?'

'Let me rest. A few minutes, by myself.'

He took her to her bedroom and eased her down on the round bed. Then he went out. Lona was surprised how quickly equilibrium returned, away from the restaurant. It had seemed to her, at the very end, that the sky itself had become a huge prying eye.

Calmer now, Lona rose, determined to shed the rest of her false glamour. She stepped under the vibraspray. Instantly her sumptuous gown vanished. She felt smaller, younger, at once. Naked, she made herself ready for bed.

She turned on a dim lamp, deactivated the rest of the room glow, and slipped between the sheets. They were cool and agreeable against her skin. A control console governed the movements and form of the bed, but Lona ignored it. She said softly into an intercom beside her pillow, 'Minner, will you come in now?'

He entered at once. He was still wearing his flamboyant dinner costume, cape and all. The flaring rib-like projections were so strange that they nearly cancelled out the other strangeness that was his body.

Dinner had been a disaster, she thought. The restaurant, so glittering, had been like a torture chamber for her. But the evening might be salvaged.

'Hold me,' she said in a thin voice. 'I'm still a little shaky, Minner.'

Burris came to her. He sat beside her, and she rose a little, letting the sheet slip down to reveal her breasts. He reached for her, but the ribs of his costume formed an unbending barrier, thwarting contact.

'I'd better get out of this rig,' he said.

'The vibraspray's over there.'

'Shall I turn off the light?'

'No. No.'

Her eyes did not leave him as he crossed the room.

He mounted the platform of the vibraspray and turned it on. It was designed to cleanse the skin of any adhering matter, and a sprayon garment would naturally be the first to go. Burris's outlandish costume disappeared.

Lona had never seen his body before.

Unflinchingly, ready for any catastrophic revelation, she watched the naked man turn to face her. Her face was rigidly set, as was his, for this was a double test, showing if she could bear the shock of facing the unknown, showing if he could bear the shock of facing her response.

She had dreaded this moment for days. But now it was here, and in spreading wonder she discovered that she had lived through and past the dreaded moment without harm.

He was not nearly so terrible to behold as she had anticipated.

Of course, he was strange. His skin, like the skin of his face and arms, was glossy and unreal, a seamless container like none ever worn by man before. He was hairless. He had neither breasts nor navel, a fact that Lona realized slowly after searching for the cause of the wrongness.

His arms and legs were attached to his body in an unfamiliar manner, and by several inches in unfamiliar places. His chest seemed too deep in proportion to the width of his

101

hips. His knees did not stand out from his legs as knees should do. When he moved, the muscles of his body rippled in a curious way.

But these were minor things, and they were not true deformities. He bore no hideous scars, no hidden extra limbs, no unexpected eyes or mouths on his body. The real changes were within, and on his face.

And the one aspect of all that had concerned Lona was anticlimatic. Against probability, he seemed normally male. So far as she could tell, at least.

Burris came toward the bed. She lifted her arms. An instant later and he was beside her, his skin against hers. The texture was strange but not unpleasant. He seemed oddly shy just now. Lona drew him closer. Her eyes closed. She did not want to see his altered face in this moment, and in any case her eyes seemed suddenly sensitive even to the faint light of the lamp. Her hand moved out to him. Her lips met his.

She had not been kissed often. But she had never been kissed like this. Those who had redesigned his lips had not intended them for kissing, and he was forced to make contact in an unwieldy way, mouth to mouth. But, again, it was not unpleasant. And then Lona felt his fingers on her flesh, six digits to each hand. His skin had a sweet, pungent odor. The light went out.

A spring within her body was coiling tighter . . . tighter . . . tighter . . .

A spring that had been coiling ever tighter for seventeen years . . . and now its force was unleashed in a single moment of tumult.

She pulled her mouth from his. Her jaws wrenched themselves apart, and a sheath of muscle quaked in her throat. A blistering image seared her: herself on an operating table, anesthetized, her body open to the probe of the men in white. She struck the image with a bolt of lightning, and it shattered and tumbled away.

She clutched at him.

At last. At last!

He would not give her babies. She sensed that, and it did not trouble her.

'Lona,' he said, his face against her clavicle, his voice coming out smothered and thick. 'Lona, Lona, Lona . . . '

There was brightness, as of an exploding sun. Her hand ran up and down his back, and just before joining the thought

102

came to her that his skin was dry, that he did not sweat at all. Then she gasped, felt pain and pleasure in one convulsive unity, and listened in amazement to the ferocious ringing cries of lust that were fleeing of their own accord from her frenzied throat.

Twenty

After Us, the Savage God

It was a post-apocalyptic era. The doom of which the prophets had chanted had never come; or, if it had, the world had lived through it into a quieter time. They had predicted the worst, a Fimbulwinter of universal discontent. An ax-age, a sword-age, a wind-age, a wolf-age, ere the world totters. But shields were not cloven, and darkness did not fall. What had happened, and why? Duncan Chalk, one of the chief beneficiaries of the new era, often pondered that pleasant question.

The swords now were plowshares.

Hunger was abolished.

Population was controlled.

Man no longer fouled his own environment in every daily act. The skies were relatively pure. The rivers ran clear. There were lakes of blue crystal, parks of bright green. Of course, the millennium had not quite arrived; there was crime, disease, hunger, even now. But that was in the dark places. For most, it was an age of ease. Those who looked for crisis looked for it in that.

Communication in the world was instantaneous. Transportation was measurably slower than that, but still fast. The planets of the local solar system, unpeopled, were being plundered of their metals, their minerals, even their gaseous blankets. The nearer stars had been reached. Earth prospered. The ideologies of poverty wither embarrassingly in a time of plenty.

Yet plenty is relative. Needs and envies remained – the materialistic urges. The deeper, darker hungers were not always gratified by thick paychecks alone, either. An era determines for itself its characteristic forms of entertainment. Chalk had been one of the shapers of those forms.

His empire of amusement stretched halfway across the system. It brought him wealth, power, the satisfaction of the ego, and – to the measure he desired it – fame. It led him indirectly to the fulfillment of his inner needs, which were generated from his own physical and psychological makeup, and which would have pressed upon him had he lived in any other era. Now, conveniently, he was in a position to take the steps that would bring him to the position he required.

He needed to be fed frequently. And his food was only partly flesh and vegetables.

From the center of his empire Chalk followed the doings of his star-crossed pair of lovers. They were en route to Antarctica now. He received regular reports from Aoudad and Nikolaides, those hoverers over the bed of love. But by this time Chalk no longer needed his flunkies to tell him what was happening. He had achieved contact and drew his own species of information from the two splintered ones he had brought together.

Just now what he drew from them was a bland wash of happiness. Useless, for Chalk. But he played his game patiently. Mutual sympathy had drawn them close, but was sympathy the proper foundation for undying love? Chalk thought not. He was willing to gamble a fortune to prove his point. They would change toward each other. And Chalk would turn his profit, so to speak.

Aoudad was on the circuit now. 'We're just arriving, sir. They're being taken to the hotel.'

'Good. Good. See that they're given every comfort.'

'Naturally.'

'But don't spend much time near them. They want to be with each other, not chivied about by chaperones. Do you follow me, Aoudad?'

'They'll have the whole Pole to themselves.'

Chalk smiled. Their tour would be a lovers' dream. It was an elegant era, and those with the right key could open door after door of pleasures. Burris and Lona would enjoy themselves.

The apocalypse could come later.

Twenty-one

And Southward Aye We Fled

'I don't understand,' Lona said. 'How can it be summer here? When we left, it was winter!'

'In the Northern Hemisphere, yes.' Burris sighed. 'But now we're below the Equator. As far below as it's possible to get. The seasons are reversed here. When we get summer, they have winter. And now it's their summer here.'

'Yes, but why?'

'It has to do with the way the Earth is tipped on its axis. As it goes around the sun, part of the planet is in a good position to get warmed by sunlight, and part isn't. If I had a globe here, I could show you.'

'If it's summer here, though, why is there so much ice?'

The thin, whining tone of her questions annoyed him even more than the questions themselves. Burris whirled suddenly. There was a spasm within his diaphragm as mysterious organs spurted their secretions of anger into his blood.

'Damn it, Lona, didn't you ever go to school?' he blazed at her.

She shrank away from him. 'Don't shout at me, Minner. Please don't shout.'

'Didn't they teach you anything?'

'I left school early. I wasn't a good student.'

'And now I'm your teacher?'

'You don't have to be,' Lona said quietly. Her eyes were too bright now. 'You don't have to be anything for me if you don't want to be.'

He was suddenly on the defensive. 'I didn't mean to shout at you.'

'But you shouted.'

'I lost patience. All those questions –'

'All those *silly* questions – isn't that what you wanted to say?'

'Let's stop it right here, Lona. I'm sorry I blew up at you. I didn't get much sleep last night, and my nerves are frayed. Let's go for a walk. I'll try to explain the seasons to you.'

'I'm not all that interested in the seasons, Minner.'

'Forget the seasons, then. But let's walk. Let's try to calm ourselves down.'

'Do you think *I* got much sleep last night, either?'

He thought it might be time to smile. 'I guess you didn't, not really.'

'But am I shouting and complaining?'

'As a matter of fact, you are. So let's quit it right here and take a relaxing walk. Yes?'

'All right,' she said sullenly. 'A summertime stroll.'

'A summertime stroll, yes.'

They slipped on light thermal wraps, hoods, gloves. The temperature was mild for this part of the world: several degrees above freezing. The Antarctic was having a heat wave. Chalk's polar hotel was only a few dozen miles from the Pole itself, lying 'north' of the Pole, as all things must, and placed out toward the direction of the Ross Shelf Ice. It was a sprawling geodesic dome, solid enough to withstand the rigors of the polar night, airy enough to admit the texture of the Antarctic.

A double exit chamber was their gateway to the ice-realm outside. The dome was surrounded by a belt of brown-bare soil ten feet wide, laid down by the builders as an insulating zone, and beyond it was the white plateau. Instantly, as Burris and the girl emerged, a burly guide rushed up to them, grinning.

'Power-sled trip, folks? Take you to the Pole in fifteen minutes! Amundsen's camp, reconstructed. The Scott Museum. Or we could go out for a look at the glaciers back the other way. You say the word, and –'

'No.'

'I understand. Your first morning here, you'd just like to stroll around a little. Can't blame you at all. Well, you just stroll all you like. And when you decide that you're ready for a longer trip – '

'Please,' Burris said. 'Can we get by?'

The guide gave him a queer look and stepped aside. Lona slipped her arm through Burris's and they walked out onto the ice. Looking back, Burris saw a figure step from the dome and call the guide aside. Aoudad. They were having an earnest conference.

'It's so beautiful here!' Lona cried.

'In a sterile way, yes. The last frontier. Almost untouched, except for a museum here and there.'

106

'And hotels.'

'This is the only one. Chalk has a monopoly.'

The sun was high overhead, looking bright but small. This close to the Pole, the summer day would seem never to end; two months of unbroken sunlight lay ahead before the long dip into darkness began. The light glittered brilliantly over the icy plateau. Everything was flat here, a mile-high sheet of whiteness burying mountains and valleys alike. The ice was firm underfoot. In ten minutes they had left the hotel far behind.

'Which way is the South Pole?' Lona asked.

'That way. Straight ahead. We'll go over there later.'

'And behind us?'

'The Queen Maud Mountains. They drop off down to the Ross Shelf. It's a big slab of ice, seven hundred feet thick, bigger than California. The early explorers made their camps on it. We'll visit Little America in a couple of days.'

'It's so flat here. The reflection of the sun is so bright.' Lona bent, scooped a handful of snow, and scattered it gaily. 'I'd love to see some penguins. Minner, do I ask too many questions? Do I chatter?'

'Should I be honest or should I be tactful?'

'Never mind. Let's just walk.'

They walked. He found the slick footing of ice peculiarly comfortable. It gave ever so slightly with each step he took, accommodating itself nicely to the modified joints of his legs. Concrete pavements were not so friendly. Burris, who had had a tense and pain-filled night, welcomed the change.

He regretted having snarled at Lona that way.

But his patience had snapped. She was strikingly ignorant, but he had known that from the start. What he had not known was how quickly her ignorance would cease to seem charming and would begin to seem contemptible.

To awake, aching and agonized, and have to submit to that thin stream of adolescent questioning . . .

Look at the other side, he told himself. He had awakened in the middle of the night, too. He had dreamed of Manipool and naturally had burst from sleep screaming. That had happened before, but never before had there been someone beside him, warm and soft, to comfort him. Lona had done that. She had not scolded him for interfering with her own sleep. She had stroked him and soothed him until the nightmare receded into

107

unreality again. He was grateful for that. She was so tender, so loving. And so stupid.

'Have you ever seen Antarctica from space?' Lona asked.

'Many times.'

'What does it look like?'

'Just as it does on maps. More or less round, with a thumb sticking out toward South America. And white. Everywhere white. You'll see it when we head for Titan.'

She nestled into the hollow of his arm as they walked. The arm-socket was adaptable; he extended it, making a comfortable harbor for her. This body had its merits.

Lona said, 'Someday I want to come back here again and see all the sights – the Pole, the museums of the explorers, the glaciers. Only I want to come with my children.'

An icicle slipped neatly through his throat.

'What children, Lona?'

'There'll be two. A boy and a girl. In about eight years, that'll be the right time to bring them.'

His eyelids flickered uncontrollably within his thermal hood. They gnashed like the ringing walls of the Symplegades. In a low, fiercely controlled voice he said, 'You ought to know, Lona, I can't give you any children. The doctors checked that part out. The internal organs simply – '

'Yes, I know. I didn't mean children that we'd have, Minner.'

He felt his bowels go spilling out onto the ice.

She went on sweetly, 'I mean the babies I have now. The ones that were taken from my body. I'm going to get two of them back – didn't I tell you?'

Burris felt oddly relieved at the knowledge that she wasn't planning to leave him for some biologically whole man. Simultaneously he was surprised at the depth of his own relief. How smugly he had assumed that any children she mentioned would be children she expected to have by him! How stunning it had been to think that she might have children by another!

But she already had a legion of children. He had nearly forgotten that.

He said, 'No, you didn't tell me. You mean it's been agreed that you're going to get some of the children to raise yourself?'

'More or less.'

'What does that mean?'

'I don't think it's really been agreed yet. But Chalk said he'd arrange it. He promised me, he gave me his word. And I

108

know he's an important enough man to be able to do it. There are so many of the babies – they can spare a couple for the real mother if she wants them. And I do. I do. Chalk said he'd get the children for me if I – if I – '

She was silent. Her mouth was round a moment, then clamped tight.

'If you what, Lona?'

'Nothing.'

'You started to say something.'

'I said, he'd get the children for me if I wanted them.'

He turned on her. 'That's not what you were going to say. We already know you want them. What did you promise Chalk in return for getting them for you?'

The spectrum of guilt rippled across her face.

'What are you hiding from me?' he demanded.

She shook her head mutely. He seized her hand, and she pulled it away. He stood over her, dwarfing her, and as always when his emotions came forth in the new body there were strange poundings and throbbings within him.

'What did you promise him?' he asked.

'Minner, you look so strange. Your face is all blotched. Red, and purple over your cheeks . . . ?'

'What was it, Lona?'

'Nothing. Nothing. All I said to him . . . , all I agreed was . . .'

'Was?'

'That I'd be nice to you.' In a small voice. 'I promised him I'd make you happy. And he'd get me some of the babies for my own. Was that wrong, Minner?'

He felt air escaping from the gigantic puncture in his chest. Chalk had arranged this? Chalk had bribed her to care for him? Chalk? *Chalk?*

'Minner, what's wrong?'

Stormwinds blew through him. The planet was tilting on its axis, rising up, crushing him, the continents breaking loose and sliding free in a massive cascade upon him.

'Don't look at me like that,' she begged.

'If Chalk hadn't offered you the babies, would you ever have come near me?' he asked tightly. 'Would you ever have touched me at all, Lona?'

Her eyes were flecked now with tears. 'I saw you in the hospital garden. I felt so sorry for you. I didn't even know who you were. I thought you were in a fire or something. Then

I met you. I love you, Minner. Chalk couldn't make me love you. He could only get me to be good to you. But that isn't love.'

He felt foolish, idiotic, shambling, a heap of animate mud. He gawked at her. She looked mystified. Then she stooped, seized snow, balled it, flung it laughing in his face. 'Stop looking so weird,' she said. 'Chase me, Minner. Chase me!'

She sprinted away from him. In a moment she was unexpectedly far away. She paused, a dark spot on the whiteness, and picked up more snow. He watched her fashion another snowball. She threw it awkwardly, from the elbow, as a girl would, but even so it carried well, landing a dozen yards from his feet.

He broke from the stupor that her careless words had cast him into. 'You can't catch me!' Lona shrilled, and he began to run, running for the first time since he had left Manipool, taking long loping strides over the carpet of snow. Lona ran, too, arms windmilling, elbows jabbing the thin, frosty air, Burris felt power flooding his limbs. His legs, which had seemed so impossible to him with their multiple jointing, now pistoned in perfect coordination, propelling him smoothly and rapidly. His heart scarcely pounded at all. On impulse, he threw back his hood and let the near-freezing air stream across his cheeks.

It took him only a few minutes of hard running to overtake her. Lona, gasping with laughter and breathlessness, swung around as he neared her, and flung herself into his arms. His momentum carried him onward five more steps before they fell. They rolled over and over, gloved hands beating the snow, and he pushed back her hood, too, and scraped a palm's-load of ice free and thrust it into her face. The ice trickled down, past her throat, into her wrap, under her clothing, along her breasts, her belly. She shrieked in wild pleasure and indignation.

'Minner! No, Minner! No!'

He thrust more snow at her. And she at him now. Convulsed with laughter, she forced it past his collar. It was so cold that it seemed to burn. Together they floundered on the snow. Then she was in his arms, and he held her tight, nailing her to the floor of the lifeless continent. It was a long while before they rose.

Twenty-two

Hence, Loathed Melancholy

He woke screaming again that night.

Lona had been expecting it. For most of the night she had been awake herself, lying beside him in the dark, waiting for the inevitable demons to take possession of him. He had been brooding, on and off, much of the evening.

The day had been pleasant enough – barring that nasty moment right at the outset. Lona wished she could call back the admission she had made: that it was Chalk who had put her up to approaching him in the first place. At least she had withheld the most damning part of all: that Nikolaides had thought of presenting the cactus, that Nikolaides had even dictated her little note. She knew now what effect such knowledge would have on Burris. But it had been stupid even to mention Chalk's promise of restoring the babies. Lona saw that clearly now. But now was too late to unspeak the words.

He had recovered from that taut moment, and they had gone off to have fun. A snowball fight, a hike in the trackless wilderness of ice. Lona had been scared when suddenly she realized that the hotel was no longer in sight. She saw flat whiteness everywhere. No trees to cast shadows, no movements of the sun to indicate directions, and no compass. They had walked miles through an unchanging landscape. 'Can we get back?' she asked, and he nodded. 'I'm tired. I'd like to go back now.' Actually she was not all that tired, but it frightened her to think of getting lost here. They turned back, or so Burris said they had done. This new direction looked just the same as the old. There was a darkness several feet long just below the snow in one place. A dead penguin, Burris told her, and she shuddered, but then the hotel miraculously appeared. If the world was flat here, she wondered, why had the hotel vanished? And Burris explained, as he had explained so many things to her (but in a more patient tone now) that the world was not really flat here, but actually nearly as curved as at any other place, so that they need walk only a very few miles for familiar landmarks to drop below the horizon. As the hotel had done.

But the hotel had returned, and their appetites were huge, and they had hearty lunches, washed down with flagon after flagon of beer. Here no one drank green cocktails with live things swimming in them. Beer, cheese, meat – that was fit food for this land of eternal winter.

They took power-sled tours that afternoon. First they went to the South Pole.

'It looks like everything else around,' Lona said.

'What did you expect?' he asked. 'A striped pole sticking out of the snow?'

So he was being sarcastic again. She saw the sorrow in his eyes that followed his crackling comment, and told herself that he had not meant to hurt her. It was natural to him, that was all. Maybe he was in such pain himself – *real* pain – that he had to keep lashing out that way.

But actually the Pole was different from the surrounding blankness of the polar plateau. There were buildings there. A circular zone around the world's bottom some twenty yards in diameter was sacrosanct, untouched. Near it was the restored or reproduced tent of the Norwegian, Roald Amundsen, who had come by dogsled to this place a century or two ago. A striped flag fluttered over the dark tent. They peered inside: nothing.

Nearby was a small building of logs. 'Why logs?' Lona asked. 'There aren't any trees in Antarctica?' For once her question was a shrewd one. Burris laughed.

The building was sacred to the memory of Robert Falcon Scott, who had followed Amundsen to the Pole and who, unlike the Norwegian, had died on the way back. Within were diaries, sleeping-bags, the odds and ends of explorers. Lona read the plaque. Scott and his men had not died here, but rather many miles away, trapped by weariness and winter gales as they plodded toward their base. All this was strictly for show. The phoniness of it bothered Lona, and she thought it bothered Burris, too.

But it was impressive to stand right at the South Pole.

'The whole world is north of us right now,' Burris told her. 'We're hanging off the bottom edge. Everything's above us from here. But we won't fall off.'

She laughed. Nevertheless, the world did not look at all unusual to her at that moment. The surrounding land stretched away to the sides, and not up and down. She tried to picture the world as it would look from a space ferry, a ball

112

hanging in the sky, and herself, smaller than an ant, standing at the bottom with her feet toward the center and her head pointed to the stars. Somewhere it made no sense to her.

There was a refreshment stand near the Pole. They kept it covered with snow to make it inconspicuous. Burris and Lona had steaming mugs of hot chocolate.

They did not visit the underground scientific base a few hundred yards away. Visitors were welcome; scientists in thick beards lived there the year round, studying magnetism and weather and such. But Lona did not care to enter a laboratory again. She exchanged glances with Burris, and he nodded, and the guide took them back on the power-sled.

It was too late in the day to go all the way to the Ross Ice Shelf. But they traveled for more than an hour northwest from the Pole, toward a chain of mountains that never got any closer, and came to a mysterious warm spot where there was no snow, only bare brown earth stained red by a crust of algae, and rocks covered with a thin coating of yellow-green lichens. Lona asked to see penguins then, and was told that at this time of the year there were no penguins in the interior except strays. 'They're water birds,' the guide said. 'They stay close to the coast and come inland only when it's time to lay their eggs.'

'But it's summer here. They ought to be nesting now.'

'They make their nests in midwinter. The baby penguins are hatched in June and July. The darkest, coldest time of the year. You want to see penguins, you sign up for the Adélie Land tour. You'll see penguins.'

Burris seemed to be in good spirits on the long sled ride back to the hotel. He teased Lona in a lighthearted way, and at one point had the guide stop the sled so they could go sliding down a glassy-smooth embankment of snow. But as they neared the lodge, Lona detected the change coming over him. It was like the onset of twilight, but this was a season of no twilight at the Pole. Burris darkened. His face grew rigid, and he stopped laughing and joking. By the time they were passing through the double doors of the lodge, he seemed like something hewn from ice.

'What's wrong?' she asked.

'Who said anything was wrong?'

'Would you like to have a drink?'

They went to the cocktail lounge. It was a big room, paneled in wood, with a real fireplace to give it that twentieth-century

113

look. Two dozen people, more or less, sat at the heavy oaken tables, talking and drinking. All of them couples, Lona noticed. This was almost entirely a honeymoon resort. Young married people came here to begin their lives in icy Antarctic purity. The skiing was said to be excellent in the mountains of Marie Byrd Land.

Heads turned their way as Burris and Lona entered. And just as quickly turned away again in a quick reflex of aversion. Oh, so sorry. Didn't mean to stare. A man with a face like yours, he probably doesn't like to be stared at. We were just looking to see if our friends the Smiths had come down for drinks.

'The demon at the wedding feast,' Burris muttered.

Lona wasn't sure she had heard it correctly. She didn't ask him to repeat.

A robot servitor took their order. She drank beer, he a filtered rum. They sat alone at a table near the edge of the room. Suddenly they had nothing to say to each other. All about them conversation seemed unnaturally loud. Talk of future holidays, of sports, of the many available tours the resort offered.

No one came over to join them.

Burris sat rigidly, his shoulders forced upright in a posture that Lona knew must hurt him. He finished his drink quickly and did not order another. Outside, the pale sun refused to set.

'It would be so pretty here if we got a romantic sunset,' Lona said. 'Streaks of blue and gold on the ice. But we won't get it, will we?'

Burris smiled. He did not answer.

There was a flow of people in and out of the room constantly. The flow swept wide around their table. They were boulders in the stream. Hands were shaken, kisses exchanged. Lona heard people making introductions. It was the sort of place where one couple could come freely up to another, strangers, and find a warm response.

No one freely came to them.

'They know who we are,' Lona said to Burris. 'They think we're celebrities, so very important that we don't want to be bothered. So they leave us alone. They don't want to seem to be intruding.'

'All right,'

114

'Why don't we go over to someone? Break the ice, show them that we're not stand-offish.'

'Let's not. Let's just sit here.'

She thought she knew what was eating at him. He was convinced they were avoiding this table because he was ugly, or at least strange. No one wanted to have to look him full in the face. And one could not very well hold a conversation staring off to one side. So the others stayed away. Was that what was troubling him? His self-consciousness returning? She did not ask. She thought she might be able to do something about that.

An hour or so before dinner they returned to their room. It was a single large enclosure with a false harshness about it. The walls were made of split logs, rough and coarse, but the atmosphere was carefully regulated and there were all the modern conveniences. He sat quietly. After a while he stood up and began to examine his legs, swinging them back and forth. His mood was so dark now that it frightened her.

She said, 'Excuse me. I'll be back in five minutes.'

'Where are you going?'

'To check on the tours they're offering for tomorrow.'

He let her go. She went down the curving corridor toward the main lobby. Midway, a giant screen was producing an aurora australis for a group of the guests. Patterns of green and red and purple shot dramatically across a neutral gray background. It looked like a scene from the end of the world.

In the lobby Lona gathered a fistful of brochures on the tours. Then she returned to the screen-room. She saw a couple who had been in the cocktail lounge. The woman was in her early twenties, blonde, with artful green streaks rising from her hairline. Her eyes were cool. Her husband, if husband he was, was an older man, near forty, wearing a costly looking tunic. A perpetual-motion ring from one of the outworlds writhed on his left hand.

Tensely Lona approached them. She smiled.

'Hello. I'm Lona Kelvin. Perhaps you noticed us in the lounge.'

She drew tight smiles, nervous ones. They were thinking, she knew, *what does she want from us?*

They gave their names. Lona did not catch them, but that did not matter.

She said, 'I thought perhaps it would be nice if the four of us sat together at dinner tonight. I think you'd find Minner very interesting. He's been to so many planets . . . '

They looked trapped. Blonde wife was nearly panicky. Suave husband deftly came to rescue.

'We'd love to . . . other arrangements . . . friends from back home . . . perhaps another night . . . '

The tables were not limited to four or even six. There was always room for a congenial addition. Lona, rebuffed, knew now what Burris had sensed hours before. They were not wanted. He was the man of the evil eye, raining blight on their festivities. Clutching her brochures, Lona hurried back to the room. Burris was by the window, looking out over the snow.

'Come go through these with me, Minner.' Her voice was pitched too high, too sharp.

'Do any of them look interesting?'

'They all do. I don't really know what's best. You do the picking.'

They sat on the bed and sorted through the glossy sheaf. There was the Adélie Land tour, half a day, to see penguins. A full day tour to the Ross Shelf Ice, including a visit to Little America and to the other explorer bases at McMurdo Sound. Special stop to see the active volcano, Mount Erebus. Or a longer tour up to the Antarctic Peninsula to see seals and sea leopards. The skiing trip to Marie Byrd Land. The coastal mountain trip through Victoria Land to Mertz Glacial Tongue. And a dozen others. They picked the penguin tour, and when they went down for dinner later, they put their names on the list.

At dinner they sat alone.

Burris said, 'Tell me about your children, Lona. Have you ever seen them?'

'Not really. Not so I could touch, except only once. Just on screens.'

'And Chalk will really get you some to raise?'

'He said he would.'

'Do you believe him?'

'What else can I do?' she asked. Her hand covered his. 'Do your legs hurt you?'

'Not really.'

Neither of them ate much. After dinner films were shown: vivid tridims of an Antarctic winter. The darkness was the darkness of death, and a death-wind scoured across the plateau, lifting the top layer of snow like a million knives.

116

Lona saw the penguins standing on their eggs, warming them. And then she saw ragged penguins driven before the gale, marching overland while a cosmic drum throbbed in the heavens and invisible hellhounds leaped on silent pads from peak to peak. The film ended with sunrise; the ice stained blood-red with the dawn of a six-month night; the frozen ocean breaking up, giant floes clashing and shattering. Most of the hotel guests went from the screening-room to the lounge. Lona and Burris went to bed. They did not make love. Lona sensed the storm building within him, and knew that it would burst forth before morning came.

They lay cradled in darkness; the window had to be opaqued to shut out the tireless sun. Lona rested on her back beside him, breathing slowly, her flank touching his. Somehow she dozed, and a poor, shallow sleep came to her. Her own phantoms visited her after a while. She awoke, sweating, to find herself naked in a strange room with a strange man next to her. Her heart was fluttering. She pressed her hands to her breasts and remembered where she was.

Burris stirred and groaned.

Gusts of wind battered the building. This was summer, Lona reminded herself. The chill seeped to her bones. She heard a distant sound of laughter. But she did not leave his side, nor did she try to sleep again.

Her eyes, dark-adjusted, watched his face. The mouth was expressive in its hinged way, sliding open, shutting, sliding again. Once his eyes did the same, but even when the lids were pulled back he saw nothing. He's back on Manipool, Lona realized. They've just landed, he and . . . and the ones with Italian names. And in a little while the Things will come for him.

Lona tried to see Manipool. The parched and reddened soil, the twisted, thorny plants. What were the cities like? Did they have roads, cars, vid-sets? Burris had never told her. All she knew was that it was a dry world, an old world, a world where the surgeons had great skill.

And now Burris screamed.

The sound began deep in his throat, a gargled, incoherent cry, and moved higher in pitch and volume as it progressed. Turning, Lona clung to him, pressing tight. Was his skin soaked with perspiration? No; impossible; it must be her own. He thrashed and kicked, sending the coverlet to the floor. She felt his muscles coiling and bulging beneath his sleek skin. He

117

could snap me in half with a quick move, she thought.

'It's all right, Minner, I'm here. I'm here. It's all right!'

'The knives . . . Prolisse . . . good God, the knives!'

'Minner!'

She did not let go of him. His left arm was dangling limply now, seemingly bending the wrong way at the elbow. He was calming. His hoarse breath was as loud as hoofbeats. Lona reached across him and turned on the light.

His face was blotched and mottled again. He blinked in that awful sidewise way of his three or four times and put his hand to his lips. Releasing him, she sat back, trembling a little. Tonight's explosion had been more violent than the one the night before.

'A drink of water?' she asked.

He nodded. He was gripping the mattress so hard she thought he would tear it.

He gulped. She said, 'Was it that bad tonight? Were they hurting you?'

'I dreamed I was watching them operate. First Prolisse, and he died. Then they carved up Malcondotto. He died. And then . . .'

'Your turn?'

'No,' he said in wonder. 'No, they put Elise on the table. They carved her open, right between the – the breasts. And lifted up part of her chest, and I saw the ribs and her heart. And they reached inside.'

'Poor Minner.' She had to interrupt him before he spilled all that filthiness over her. Why had he dreamed of Elise? Was it a good sign, that he should see her being mutilated? Or would it have been better, she thought, if I was the one he dreamed about . . . I, being turned into something like him?

She took his hand and let it rest on the warmth of her body. There was only one method she could think of for easing his pain, and she employed it. He responded, rising, covering her. They moved urgently and harmoniously.

He appeared to sleep after that. Lona, edgier, pulled away from him and waited until a light slumber once more enveloped her. It was stained by sour dreams. It seemed that a returning starman had brought a pestilent creature with him, some kind of plump vampire, and it was affixed to her body, draining her . . . depleting her. It was a nasty dream, though not nasty enough to awaken her, and in time she passed into a deeper repose.

When they woke, there were dark circles under her eyes, and her face looked pinched and hollow. Burris showed no effects of his broken night; his skin was not capable of reacting that graphically to short-range catabolic effects. He seemed almost cheerful as he got himself ready for the new day.

'Looking forward to the penguins?' he asked her.

Had he forgotten his bleak depression of the evening and his screaming terrors of the night? Or was he just trying to sweep them from view?

Just how human is he, anyway, Lona wondered?

'Yes,' she said coolly. 'We'll have a grand time, Minner. I can't wait to see them.'

Twenty-three
The Music of the Spheres

'They're beginning to hate each other already,' Chalk said pleasantly.

He was alone, but to him that was no reason for not voicing his thoughts. He often talked to himself. A doctor once had told him that there were positive neuropsychic benefits to be had from vocalizing, even in solitude.

He floated in a bath of aromatic salts. The tub was ten feet deep, twenty feet long, a dozen feet wide: ample room even for the bulk of a Duncan Chalk. Its marble sides were flanked by alabaster rims and a surrounding tilework of shimmering ox-blood porcelain, and the whole bathing enclosure was covered by a thick, clear dome that gave Chalk a full view of the sky. There was no reciprocal view of Chalk for an outsider; an ingenious optical engineer had seen to that. From without, the dome presented a milky surface streaked with whorls of light pink.

Chalk drifted idly, gravity-free, thinking of his suffering *amanti*. Night had fallen, but there were no stars tonight, only the reddish haze of unseen clouds. It was snowing once more. The flakes performed intricate arabesques as they spiraled toward the surface of the dome.

'He is bored with her,' Chalk said. 'She is afraid of him. She lacks intensity, to his taste. For hers, his voltage is too high. But they travel together. They eat together. They sleep together. And soon they'll quarrel bitterly.'

The tapes were very good. Aoudad, Nikolaides, both of them remaining surreptitiously close behind, picking up scattered gay images of the pair to relay to a waiting public. That snowball fight; a masterpiece. And the power-sled trip. Minner and Lona at the South Pole. The public was eating it up.

Chalk, in his own way, ate it up, too.

He closed his eyes and opaqued his dome and drifted easily in the warm, fragrant tub. To him came splintered, fragmented sensations of disquiet.

. . . to have joints that did not behave as human joints should . . .

. . . to feel despised, rejected of mankind . . .

. . . childless motherhood . . .

. . . bright flashes of pain, bright as the thermoluminescent fungi casting their yellow glow on his office walls . . .

. . . the ache of the body and the ache of the soul . . .

. . . alone!

. . . unclean!

Chalk gasped as though a low current were running through his body. A finger flew up at an angle to his hand and remained there a moment. A hound with slavering jaws bounded through his forebrain. Beneath the sagging flesh of his chest the thick bands of muscle rhythmically contracted and let go.

. . . demon-visits in the sleep . . .

. . . a forest of watching eyes, stalked and shining . . .

. . . a world of dryness . . . thorns . . . thorns . . .

. . . the click and scratch of strange beasts moving in the walls . . . dry rot of the soul . . . all poetry turned to ash, all love to rust . . .

. . . stony eyes lifted toward the universe . . . and the universe peering back . . .

In ecstasy Chalk kicked at the water, sending up spewing cascades. He slapped its surface with the flat of his hand. Flukes! There go flukes! Ahoy, ahoy!

Pleasure engulfed and consumed him.

And this, he told himself cozily some minutes later, was merely the beginning.

Twenty-four

In Heaven as it is on Earth

On a day of flaming sunlight they left for Luna Tivoli, entering the next stage of their passage through Chalk's aeries of delight. The day was bright, but it was still winter; they were fleeing from the true winter of the north and the wintry summer of the south to the weatherless winter of the void. At the spaceport they received the full celebrity treatment: newsreel shots in the terminal, then the snub-snouted little car rushing them across the field while the common folk looked on in wonder, vaguely cheering the notables, whoever they might be.

Burris hated it. Every stray glance at him now seemed fresh surgery on his soul.

'Why did you let yourself in for it, then?' Lona wanted to know. 'If you don't want people to see you like this, why did you ever let Chalk send you on this trip?'

'As a penance. As a deliberately chosen atonement for my withdrawal from the world. For the sake of discipline.'

The string of abstractions failed to convince her. Perhaps they made no impact at all.

'But didn't you have a *reason*?'

'Those were my reasons.'

'Just words.'

'Never scoff at words, Lona.'

Her nostrils flared momentarily. 'You're making fun of me again!'

'Sorry.' Genuinely. It was so easy to mock her.

She said, 'I know what it's like to be stared at. I'm shy about it. But I had to do this, so Chalk would give me some of my babies.'

'He promised me something, too.'

'There! I knew you'd admit it!'

'A body transplant,' Burris confessed. 'He'll put me into a healthy, normal human body. All I have to do is let his cameras dissect me for a few months.'

'Can they really do a thing like that?'

121

'Lona, if they can make a hundred babies from a girl who's never been touched by a man, they can do anything.'

'But . . . to switch bodies . . .'

Wearily he said, 'They haven't perfected the technique yet. It may be a few more years. I'll have to wait.'

'Oh, Minner, that would be wonderful! To put you in a real body!'

'This is my real body.'

'*Another* body. That isn't so different. That doesn't hurt you so much. If they only could!'

'If they only could, yes.'

She was more excited about it than he was. He had lived with the idea for weeks, long enough to doubt that it would ever be possible. And now he had dangled it before her, a gleaming new toy. But what did she care? They weren't married. She'd get her babies from Chalk as her reward for this antic and would disappear into obscurity once more, fulfilled after her fashion, glad to be rid of that irritating, chafing, sarcastic consort. He'd go his own way, too, perhaps condemned to this grotesque housing forever, perhaps transferred to a sleek standard model body.

The car scooted up a ramp, and they were within the ship. The vehicle's top sprang back. Bart Aoudad peered in at them.

'How are the lovebirds?'

A silent exit, unsmiling. Aoudad, worried, fluttered about them. 'Everybody cheerful, relaxed? No spacesickness, eh, Minner? Not you! Hah-hah-hah!'

'Hah,' said Burris.

Nikolaides, too, was there, with documents, booklets, expense vouchers. Dante had needed only Virgil to guide him through the circles of Hell, but I get two. We live in inflationary times. Burris gave Lona his arm, and they moved toward the innerness of the ship. Her fingers were rigid against his flesh. She was nervous about going to space, he thought, or else the unbroken tension of this grand tour was weighing too heavily on her.

It was a brief trip: eight hours under low but steady acceleration to cover the 240,000 miles. This same ship had once made it in two stops, pausing first at the pleasure-satellite orbiting 50,000 miles from Earth. But the pleasure-satellite had exploded ten years ago, in one of the rare miscalculations of a secure epoch. Thousands of lives lost; debris raining down on Earth for a month; bare girders of the shattered globe orbiting

122

like bones of a giant nearly three years before the salvage operation was complete.

Someone Burris had loved had been aboard the Wheel when it died. She was there with someone else, though, savoring the game tables, the sensory shows, the haute cuisine, the atmosphere of never-come-tomorrow. Tomorrow had come unexpectedly.

He had thought, when she broke with him, that nothing worse could happen to him in the rest of his days. A young man's romantic fantasy, for very shortly she was dead, and that was far worse for him than when she had refused him. Dead, she was beyond hope of reclaiming, and for a while he was dead, too, though still walking about. And after that, curiously, the pain ebbed until it was all gone. The worst possible thing, to lose a girl to a rival, then to lose her to catastrophe? Hardly. Hardly. Ten years later Burris had lost himself. Now he thought he knew what the real worst might be.

'Ladies and gentlemen, welcome aboard *Aristarchus IV*. On behalf of Captain Villeparisis, I want to offer our best wishes for a pleasant trip. We must ask you to remain in your cradles until the period of maximum acceleration is over. Once we've escaped from Earth, you'll be free to stretch your legs a bit and enjoy a view of space.'

The ship held four hundred passengers, freight, mail. There were twenty private cabins along its haunches, and one had been assigned to Burris and Lona. The others sat side by side in a vast congregation, wriggling for a view of the nearest port.

'Here we go,' Burris said softly.

He felt the jets flail and kick at the earth; felt the rockets cut in, felt the ship lift effortlessly. A triple bank of gravitrons shielded the passengers from the worst effects of the blast-off, but it was impossible to delete gravity altogether on so huge a vessel, as Chalk had been able to do on his little pleasure-craft.

The shrinking Earth dangled like a green plum just outside the viewport. Burris realized that Lona was not looking at it, but solicitously was studying him.

'How do you feel?' she asked.

'Fine. Fine.'

'You don't look relaxed.'

'It's the gravity drag. Do you think I'm nervous about going into space?'

A shrug. 'It's your first time up since – since Manipool, isn't it?'

123

'I took that ride in Chalk's ship, remember?'

'That was different. That was sub-atmospheric.'

'You think I'm going to congeal in terror just because I'm taking a space journey?' he asked. 'Do you suppose that I imagine this ferry is a nonstop express back to Manipool?'

'You're twisting my words.'

'Am I, now? I said I felt fine. And you began to construct a great elaborate fantasy of malaise for me. You –'

'Stop it, Minner.'

Her eyes were bleak. Her words were sharply accented, brittle, keen-edged. He forced his shoulders back against the cradle and tried to compel his hand-tentacles to uncoil. Now she had done it: he had been relaxed, but she had made him tense. Why did she have to mother him this way? He was no cripple. He didn't need to be calmed in a blast-off. He had been blasting off years before she was born. Then what frightened him now? How could her words have undermined his confidence so easily?

They halted the quarrel as though slicing a tape, but ragged edges remained. He said, as gently as he could, 'Don't miss the view, Lona. You've never seen Earth from up here before, have you?'

The planet was far from them now. Its complete outline could be discerned. The Western Hemisphere faced them in a blaze of sunlight. Of Antarctica, where they had been only hours ago, nothing was visible except the long jutting finger of the Peninsula, thumbing itself at Cape Horn.

With an effort not to sound didactic, Burris showed her how the sunlight struck the planet athwart, warming the south at this time of year, barely brightening the north. He spoke of the ecliptic and its plane, of the rotation and revolution of the planet, of the procession of the seasons. Lona listened gravely, nodding often, making polite sounds of agreement whenever he paused to await them. He suspected that she still did not understand. But at this point he was willing to settle for the shadow of comprehension, if he could not have the substance, and she gave him the shadow.

They left their cabin and toured the ship. They saw the Earth from various angles. They bought drinks. They were fed. Aoudad, from his seat in the tourist section, smiled at them. They were stared at considerably.

In the cabin once more, they dozed.

They slept through the mystic moment of turnover, when

they passed from Earth's grasp at last into Luna's. Burris woke joltingly, staring across the sleeping girl and blinking at the blackness. It seemed to him that he saw the charred girders of the shattered Wheel drifting out there. No, no; impossible. But he *had* seen them, on a journey a decade ago. Some of the bodies that had spilled from the Wheel as it split open were said still to be in orbit, moving in vast parabolas about the sun. To Burris's knowledge, no one had actually seen such a wanderer in years; most of the corpses, perhaps nearly all, had been decently collected by torch-ships and carried off, and the rest, he would like to believe, had by this time made their way to the sun for the finest of all funerals. It was an old private terror of his to see her contorted face come drifting up within view as she passed through this zone.

The ship heeled and pivoted gently, and the beloved white pocked countenance of the Moon came into view.

Burris touched Lona's arm. She stirred, blinked, looked at him, then outward. Watching her, he detected the spreading wonder on her face even with her back to him.

Half a dozen shining domes now could be seen on Luna's surface.

'Tivoli!' she cried.

Burris doubted that any of the domes really was the amusement park. Luna was infested with domed buildings, built over the decades for a variety of warlike, commercial, or scientific reasons, and none of these matched his own mental picture of Tivoli. He did not correct her, though. He was learning.

The ferry, decelerating, spiraled down to its landing pad.

This was an age of domes, many of them the work of Duncan Chalk. On Earth they tended to be trussed geodesic domes, but not always; here, under lessened gravity, they usually were the simpler, less rigid extruded domes of one-piece construction. Chalk's empire of pleasure was bounded and delimited by domes, beginning with the one over his private pool, and then on to the cupola of the Galactic Room, the Antarctic hostelry, the Tivoli dome, and outward, outward to the stars.

The landing was smooth.

'Let's have a good time here, Minner! I've always dreamed of coming here!'

'We'll enjoy ourselves,' he promised.

Her eyes glittered. A child – no more than that – she was. Innocent, enthusiastic, simple – he ticked off her qualities. But she was warm. She cherished and nourished and mothered him,

to a fault. He knew he was underestimating her. Her life had
known so little pleasure that she had not grown jaded with
small thrills. She could respond openly and wholeheartedly to
Chalk's parks. She was young. But not hollow, Burris tried to
persuade himself. She had suffered. She bore scars, even as he
did.

The ramp was down. She rushed from the ship into the waiting dome, and he followed her, having only a little trouble
coordinating his legs.

Twenty-five

Tears of the Moon

Lona watched breathlessly as the cannon recoiled and the
cartridge of fireworks went sliding up, up the shaft, through
the aperture in the dome, and out into the blackness. She held
her breath. The cartridge exploded.

Color stained the night.

There was no air out there, nothing to cushion the particles
of powder as they drifted down. They did not drift, even, but
remained more or less where they were. The pattern was bril-
liant. They were doing animals now. The strange figures of
extraterrestrial figures. Beside her, Burris stared upward as
intently as anyone else.

'Have you ever seen one of those?' she asked.

It was a creature with ropy tendrils, an infinite neck, flat-
tened paddles for feet. Some swampy world had spawned it.

'Never.'

A second cartridge shot aloft. But this was only the oblitera-
tor, cleansing away the paddle-footed one and leaving the
heavenly blackboard blank for the next image.

Another shot.

Another.

Another.

'It's so different from fireworks on Earth,' she said. 'No
boom. No blast. And then everything just stays there. If they
didn't blot it out, how long would it stay, Minner?'

'A few minutes. There's gravity here, too. The particles would get pulled down. And disarranged by cosmic debris. All sorts of garbage comes peppering in from space.'

He was always ready for any question, always had an answer. At first that quality had awed her. Now it was an irritant. She wished she could stump him. She kept on trying. Her questions, she knew, annoyed him just about as much as his answers annoyed her.

A fine pair we are. Not even honeymooners yet, and already setting little traps for each other!

They watched the silent fireworks for half an hour. Then she grew restless, and they moved away.

'Where to now?' he asked.

'Let's just wander.'

He was tense and jittery. She felt it, sensed him ready to leap for her throat if she blundered. How he must hate being here in this silly amusement park! They were staring at him a lot. At her, too, but she was interesting for what had been done with her, not for the way she looked, and the eyes did not linger long.

They moved on, down one corridor of booths and up the next.

It was a carnival of the traditional sort, following a pattern set centuries ago. The technology had changed, but not the essence. Here were games of skill and Kewpie dolls; cheap restaurants selling dished-up dross; whirling rides to suit any dervish; sideshows of easy horror; dance halls; gambling pavilions; darkened theaters (adults only!) in which to reveal the sagging mysteries of the flesh; the flea circus and the talking dog; fireworks, however mutated; blaring music; blazing stanchions of light. A thousand acres of damp delight, done up in the latest trickery. The most significant difference between Chalk's Luna Tivoli and a thousand tivolis of the past was its location, in the broad bosom of Copernicus Crater, looking toward the eastern arc of the ringwall. One breathed pure air here, but one danced in fractional gravity. This was Luna.

'Whirlpool?' a sinuous voice asked. 'Take the Whirlpool, mister, miss?'

Lona pressed forward, smiling. Burris slapped coins onto the counter and they were admitted. A dozen aluminum shells gaped like the remains of giant clams, floating on a quicksilver lake. A squat, bare-chested man with coppery skin said, 'Shell for two? This way, this way!'

Burris helped her into one of the shells. He sat beside her. The top was sealed in place. It was dark, warm, oppressively close inside. There was just room for the two of them.

'Happy womb fantasies,' he said.

She took his hand and held it grimly. Through the quick-silver lake came a spark of motivating power. Away they went, skimming on the unknown. Down what black tunnels, through what hidden gorges? The shell rocked in a maelstrom. Lona screamed, again, again, again.

'Are you afraid?' he asked.

'I don't know. It moves so fast!'

'We can't get hurt.'

It was like floating, like flying. Virtually no gravity, and no friction to impede their squirting motion as they slid hither and yon down the byways and cloacae of the ride. Secret petcocks opened, and scent filtered in.

'What do you smell?' she asked him.

'The desert. The smell of heat. And you?'

'The woods on a rainy day. Rotting leaves, Minner. How can that be?'

Maybe his senses don't pick up things the way mine do, the way a human's do. How can he smell the desert? That ripe, rich odor of mold and dampness! She could see red toadstools bursting from the ground. Small things with many legs scutter-ing and burrowing. A shining worm. And he: the desert?

The shell seemed to flip over, strike its supporting medium flat on, and right itself. The scent had changed by the time Lona noticed it again.

'Now it's the Arcade at night,' she said. 'Popcorn . . . sweat . . . laughter. What does laughter smell like, Minner? What does it seem like to you?'

'The fuel-room of a ship at core-changing time. Something was burning a few hours ago. Frying fat where the rods leaked. It hits you like a nail rammed up the nostril.'

'How can it be that we don't smell the same things?'

'Olfactory psychovariation. We smell the things that our minds trigger for us. They aren't giving us any particular scent, just the raw material. We shape the patterns.'

'I don't understand, Minner.'

He was silent. More odors came: hospital-smell, moonlight-smell, steel-smell, snow-smell. She did not ask him about his own responses to this generalized stimulation. Once he gasped; once he winced and dug fingertips into her thigh.

128

The barrage of odors ceased.

Still the sleek shell slipped on, minute after minute. Now came sounds: tiny pinging bursts, great organ throbs, hammer blows, rhythmic scraping of rasp on rasp. They missed no sense here. The interior of the shell grew cool, and then warm again; the humidity varied in a complex cycle. Now the shell zigged, now it zagged. It whirled dizzyingly, a final frenzy of motion, and abruptly they were safe at harbor. His hand engulfed hers as he pulled her forth.

'Fun?' he asked unsmilingly.

'I'm not sure. Unusual, anyway.'

He bought her cotton candy. They passed a booth where one flipped little glass globes at golden targets on a moving screen. Hit the target three out of four, win a prize. Men with Earthside muscles struggled to cope with the low gravity and failed, while pouting girls stood by. Lona pointed at the prizes: subtle alien designs, abstract rippling forms executed in furry cloth. 'Win me one, Minner!' she begged.

He paused and watched the men making their hapless looping tosses. Most far overshot the target; some, compensating, flipped feebly and saw their marbles droop slowly short of the goal. The crowd at the booth was closely packed as he moved among them, but the onlookers gave way for him, uneasily edging away. Lona noticed it and hoped he did not. Burris put down money and picked up his marbles. His first shot was off the mark by six inches.

'Nice try, buddy! Give him room! Here's one who's got the range!' The huckster behind the boothfront peered disbelievingly at Burris's face. Lona reddened. Why do they have to stare? Does he look that strange?

He tossed again. *Clang.* Then: *clang. Clang.*

'Three in a row! Give the little lady her prize!'

Lona clutched something warm, furry, almost alive. They moved away from the booth, escaping a buzz of talk. Burris said, 'There are things to respect about this hateful body, Lona.'

Some time later she put the prize down, and when she turned for it, it had disappeared. He offered to win her another, but she told him not to worry about it.

They did not enter the building of the flesh shows.

When they came to the freak house, Lona hesitated, wanting to go inside but uncertain about suggesting it. The hesitation was fatal. Three beer-blurred faces emerged, looked at Burris, guffawed.

'Hey! There's one that escaped!'

Lona recognized the fiery blotches of fury on his cheeks. She steered him quickly away, but the wound had been made. How many weeks of self-repair undone in a moment?

The night pivoted around that point. Up till then he had been tolerant, faintly amused, only slightly bored. Now he became hostile. She saw his eye-shutters pull back to their full opening, and the cold glare of those revealed eyes would have eaten like acid into this playland if it could. He walked stiffly. He grudged every new moment here.

'I'm tired, Lona. I want to go to the room.'

'A little while longer.'

'We can come back tomorrow night.'

'But it's still early, Minner!'

His lips did odd things. 'Stay here by yourself, then.'

'No! I'm afraid! I mean – what fun would it be without you?'

'I'm not having fun.'

'You seemed to be . . . before.'

'That was before. This is now.' He plucked at her sleeve. 'Lona –'

'No,' she said. 'You aren't taking me away so fast. There's nothing to do in the room but sleep and have sex and look at the stars. This is Tivoli, Minner. *Tivoli!* I want to drink up every minute of it.'

He said something she could not make out, and they moved on to a new section of the park. But his restlessness mastered him. In a few minutes he was asking again that they go.

'Try to enjoy yourself, Minner.'

'This place is making me sick. The noise . . . the smell . . . the *eyes*.'

'No one's looking at you.'

'Very funny! Did you hear what they said when –'

'They were drunk.' He was begging for sympathy, and for once she was tired of giving it to him. 'Oh, I know, your feelings are hurt. Your feelings get hurt so easily. Well, for once stop feeling so sorry for yourself! I'm here to have a good time, and you're not going to spoil it!'

'Viciousness!'

'No worse than selfishness!' she snapped at him.

Overhead the fireworks went off. A garish serpent with seven tails sprawled across the heavens.

'How much longer do you want to stay?' Steely now.

'I don't know. Half an hour. An hour.'

'Fifteen minutes?'

'Let's not bargain over it. We haven't seen a tenth of what's here yet.'

'There are other nights.'

'Back to that again. Minner, stop it! I don't want to quarrel with you, but I'm not giving in. I'm just not giving in.'

He made a courtly bow, dipping lower than anyone with human skeletal structure could possibly have done. 'At your service, milady.' The words were venomous. Lona chose to ignore the venom and took him onward down the cluttered path. It was the worst quarrel they had had so far. In past frictions they had been cool, snippy, sarcastic, withdrawn. But never had they stood nose to nose, barking at each other. They had even drawn a small audience: Punch and Judy hollering it up for the benefit of interested onlookers. What was happening? Why were they bickering? Why, she wondered, did it sometimes seem as though he hated her? Why did she feel at those times that it could be quite easy to hate him?

They should be giving each other support. That was how it had been at the beginning. A bond of shared sympathy had linked them, for they both had suffered. What had happened to that? So much bitterness had crept into things now. Accusations, recriminations, tensions.

Before them, three intersecting yellow wheels performed an intricate dance of flame. Pulsating lights bobbed and flickered. High on a pillar a nude girl appeared, draped in living glow. She waved, beckoned, a muezzin calling the faithful to the house of lust. Her body was improbably feminine; her breasts were jutting shelves, her buttocks were giant globes. No one was born like that. She must have been changed by doctors . . .

A member of our club, thought Lona. Yet she doesn't mind. She's up there in front of everybody and happy to draw her pay. What's it like at four in the morning for her? Does she mind?

Burris was staring fixedly at the girl.

'It's just meat,' Lona said. 'Why are you so fascinated?'

'That's Elise up there!'

'You're mistaken, Minner. She wouldn't be here. Certainly not up there.'

'I tell you it's Elise. My eyes are sharper than yours. You hardly know what she looks like. They've done something to her body, they've padded her somehow, but I know it's Elise!'

'Go to her, then.'

He stood frozen. 'I didn't say I wanted to.'

'You just thought it.'

'Now you're jealous of a naked girl on a pillar?'

'You loved her before you ever knew me.'

'I never loved her,' he shouted, and the lie emblazoned itself on his forehead.

From a thousand loudspeakers came a paean of praise for the girl, for the park, for the visitors. All sound converged toward a single shapeless roar. Burris moved closer to the pillar. Lona followed him. The girl was dancing now, kicking up her heels, capering wildly. Her bare body gleamed. The swollen flesh quivered and shook. She was all carnality in a single vessel.

'It's not Elise,' said Burris suddenly, and the spell broke.

He turned away, his face darkening, and halted. All about them, fair-goers were streaming toward the pillar, the focal point of the park now, But Lona and Burris did not move. Their backs were to the dancer. Burris jerked as if struck, and folded his arms across his chest. He sank to a bench, head down.

This was no snobbery or boredom. He was sick, she realized.

'I feel so tired,' he said huskily. 'Drained of strength. I feel a thousand years old, Lona!'

Reaching for him, she coughed. Quite suddenly tears were streaming from her eyes. She dropped down beside him on the bench, struggling for breath.

'I feel the same way. Worn out.'

'What's happening?'

'Something we breathed on that ride? Something we ate, Minner?'

'No. Look at my hands.'

They were shaking. The little tentacles were hanging limp. His face was gray.

And she: it was as though she had run a hundred miles tonight. Or been delivered of a hundred babies.

This time, when he suggested that they leave the amusement park, she did not quarrel with him.

Twenty-six

Frost at Midnight

On Titan she broke away and left him. Burris had seen it coming for days and was not at all surprised. It came as something of a relief.

Tension had been rising since the South Pole. He was not sure why, other than that they were unfit for each other. But they had been at each other's throats steadily, first in a hidden way, then openly but figuratively and at the last literally. So she went away from him.

They spent six days at Luna Tivoli. The pattern of each day was the same. Late rising, a copious breakfast, some viewing of the Moon, and then to the park. The place was so big that there were always new discoveries to be made, yet by the third day Burris found that they were compulsively retracing their steps, and by the fifth he was enduringly sick of Tivoli. He tried to be tolerant, since Lona took such obvious pleasure in the place. But eventually his patience wore thin, and they quarreled. Each night's quarrel exceeded in intensity the one of the night before. Sometimes they resolved the conflict in fierce, sweaty passion, sometimes in sleepless nights of sulking.

And always, during or just after the quarrel, came that feeling of fatigue, that sickening, destructive loss of stamina. Nothing like that had ever happened to Burris before. The fact that the fits came over the girl simultaneously made it doubly strange. They said nothing to Aoudad and Nikolaides, whom they occasionally saw on the fringes of the crowds.

Burris knew that the virulent arguments were driving an ever-wider wedge between them. In less stormy moments he regretted that, for Lona was tender and kind, and he valued her warmth. All that was forgotten in his moments of rage, though. Then she seemed empty and useless and maddening to him, a burden added to all his other burdens, a foolish and ignorant and hateful child. He told her all that, at first hiding his meaning behind blunting metaphors, later hurling the naked words.

A breakup had to come. They were exhausting themselves,

133

depleting their vital substances in these battles. The moments of love were more widely spaced now. Bitterness broke in more often.

On the arbitrarily designated morning of their arbitrarily designated sixth day at Luna Tivoli, Lona said, 'Let's cancel and go on to Titan now.'

'We're supposed to spend five more days here.'

'Do you really want to?'

'Well, frankly . . . no.'

He was afraid it would provoke another fountain of angry words, and it was too early in the day for them to begin that. But no, this was her morning for sacrificial gestures. She said, 'I think I've had enough, and it's no secret that you've had enough. So why should we stay? Titan's probably much more exciting.'

'Probably.'

'And we've been so bad to each other here. A change of scenery ought to help.'

It certainly would. Any barbarian with a fat wallet could afford the price of a ticket to Luna Tivoli, and the place was full of boors, drunks, rowdies. It drew liberally on a potential audience that went far deeper than Earth's managerial classes. But Titan was more select. Only wealthy sophisticates comprised its clientele, those to whom spending twice a workingman's annual wage on a single short trip was trivial. Such people, at least, would have the courtesy to deal with him as though his deformities did not exist. Antarctica's honeymooners, shutting their eyes to all that troubled them, had simply treated him as invisible. Luna Tivoli's patrons had guffawed in his face and mocked his differentness. On Titan, though, innate good manners would decree a cool indifference to his appearance. Look upon the strange man, smile, chat gracefully, but never show by word or deed that you are aware he is strange: that was good breeding. Of the three cruelties, Burris thought he preferred that kind.

He cornered Aoudad by the glare of fireworks and said, 'We've had enough here. Book us for Titan.'

'But you have –'

' – another five days. Well, we don't want them. Get us out of here and to Titan.'

'I'll see what I can do,' Aoudad promised.

Aoudad had watched them quarrel. Burris felt unhappy about that, for reasons which he despised. Aoudad and Nikolaides had been Cupids to them, and Burris somehow held himself responsible for behaving at all times like an enthralled lover. Obscurely, he failed Aoudad whenever he snarled at Lona. Why do I give a damn about failing Aoudad? Aoudad isn't complaining about the quarrels. He doesn't offer to mediate. He doesn't say a word.

As Burris expected, Aoudad got them tickets to Titan without any difficulty. He called ahead to notify the resort that they would be arriving ahead of schedule. And off they went.

A lunar blast-off was nothing like a departure from Earth. With only a sixth the gravity to deal with, it took just a gentle shove to send the ship into space. This was a bustling spaceport, with departures daily for Mars, Venus, Titan, Ganymede, and Earth, every third day for the outer planets, weekly for Mercury. No interstellar ships left from Luna; by law and custom, starships could depart only from Earth, monitored every step of the way until they made the leap into warp somewhere beyond Pluto's orbit. Most of the Titan-bound ships stopped first at the important mining center on Ganymede, and their original itinerary had called for them to take one of those. But today's ship was nonstop. Lona would miss Ganymede, but it was her own doing. She had suggested the early arrival, not he. Perhaps they could stop at Ganymede on the way back to Earth.

There was a forced cheeriness about Lona's chatter as they slid into the gulf of darkness. She wanted to know all about Titan, just as she had wanted to know all about the South Pole, the change of seasons, the workings of a cactus, and many other things; but those questions she had asked out of naïve curiosity, and these were asked in the hope of rebuilding contact, any contact, between herself and him.

It would not work, Burris knew.

'It's the biggest moon in the system. It's bigger even than Mercury, and Mercury's a planet.'

'But Mercury goes around the sun, and Titan goes around Saturn.'

'That's right. Titan's much larger than our own moon. It's about seven hundred and fifty thousand miles from Saturn. You'll have a good view of the rings. It has an atmosphere: methane, ammonia, not very good for the lungs. Frozen. They say it's picturesque. I've never been there.'

'How come?'

'When I was young, I couldn't afford to go. Later I was too busy in other parts of the universe.'

The ship slipped on through space. Lona stared, wide-eyed, as they hopped over the plane of the asteroid belt, got a decent view of Jupiter not too far down its orbit from them, and sped outward. Saturn was in view.

To Titan then they came.

A dome again, of course. A bleak landing pad on a bleak plateau. This was a world of ice, but far different from deathly Antarctica. Every inch of Titan was alien and strange, while in Antarctica everything quickly became grindingly familiar. This was no simple place of cold and wind and whiteness.

There was Saturn to consider. The ringed planet hung low in the heavens, considerably larger than Earth appeared from Luna. There was just enough methane-ammonia atmosphere to give Titan's sky a bluish tinge, creating a handsome backdrop for glowing, golden Saturn with his thick, dark atmospheric stripe and his Midgard serpent of tiny particles.

'The ring is so thin,' Lona complained. 'Edge-on like this, I can hardly see it!'

'It's thin because Saturn's so big. We'll have a better view of it tomorrow. You'll see that it isn't one ring but several. The inner rings move faster than the outer ones.'

So long as he kept conversation on that sober level, all went well. But he hesitated to deviate from the impersonal, and so did she. Their nerves were too raw. They stood too close to the edge of the abyss after their recent quarrels.

They occupied one of the finest rooms in the glistening hotel. All about them were the moneyed ones, Earth's highest caste, those who had made fortunes in planetary development or warp-transport or power systems. Everyone seemed to know everyone else. The women, whatever their ages, were slim, agile, alert. The men were often beefy, but they moved with strength and vigor. No one made rude remarks about Burris or about Lona. No one stared. They were all friendly, in their distant way.

At dinner, the first night, they were joined at table by an industrialist with large holdings on Mars. He was far into his seventies, with a tanned, seamed face and narrow dark eyes. His wife could not have been more than thirty. They talked mostly of the commercial exploitation of extrasolar planets.

Lona, afterward: 'She has her eye on you!'

'She didn't let me know about that.'

'It was awfully obvious. I bet she was touching your foot under the table.'

He sensed a struggle coming on. Hastily he led Lona to a viewport in the dome. 'I tell you what,' he said. 'If she seduces me, you have my permission to seduce her husband.'

'Very amusing.'

'What's wrong? He has money.'

'I haven't been in this place half a day and I hate it already.'

'Stop it, Lona. You're pushing your imagination too hard. That woman wouldn't touch me. The thought would give her the shudders for a month, believe me. Look, look out there.'

A storm was blowing up. Harsh winds ripped against the dome. Saturn was nearly in the full phase tonight, and his reflected light made a glitterng track across the snow, meeting and melding with the white glare of the dome's illuminated ports. The precise needle-tips of stars were strewn across the vault of sky, looking nearly as hard as they would appear from space itself.

It was starting to snow.

They watched the wind whipping the snow about for a while. Then they heard music and followed it. Most of the guests were moving along the same track.

'Do you want to dance?' Lona asked.

An orchestra in evening clothes had appeared from somewhere. The tinkling, swirling sounds rose in volume. Strings, winds, a bit of percussion, a sprinkling of the alien instruments so popular in big-band music nowadays. The elegant guests moved in graceful rhythms over a shining floor.

Stiffly Burris took Lona in his arms and they joined the dancers.

He had never danced much before, and not at all since his return to Earth from Manipool. The mere thought of dancing in a place like this would have seemed grotesque to him only a few months ago. But he was surprised how well his re-designed body caught the rhythms of it. He was learning grace in these elaborate new bones. Around, around, around . . .

Lona's eyes held firm on his. She was not smiling. She seemed afraid of something.

Overhead was another clear dome. The Duncan Chalk school of architecture: show 'em the stars, but keep 'em warm. Gusts of wind sent snowflakes skidding across the top of the dome and drove them just as swiftly away. Lona's hand was cold in his. The tempo of the dance increased. The thermal regulators within him that had replaced his sweat glands were working overtime. Could he keep to such a giddy pace? Would he stumble?

The music stopped.

The dinnertime couple came over. The woman smiled. Lona glared.

The woman said, with the assurance of the very rich, 'May we have the next dance?'

He had tried to avoid it. Now there was no tactful way to refuse, and Lona's jealousies would get another helping of fuel. The thin, reedy sound of the oboe summoned the dancers to the floor. Burris took the woman, leaving Lona, frozen-faced, with the aging industrial baron.

The woman was a dancer. She seemed to fly over the floor. She spurred Burris to demonic exertions, and they moved around the outside of the hall, virtually floating. At that speed even his split-perception eyes failed him, and he could not find Lona. The music deafened him. The woman's smile was too bright.

'You make a wonderful partner,' she told him. 'There's a strength about you . . . a feeling for the rhythm . . . '

'I was never much of a dancer before Manipool.'

'Manipool?'

'The planet where I . . . where they . . . '

She didn't know. He had assumed everyone here was familiar with his story. But perhaps these rich ones paid no heed to current vid-program sensations. They had not followed his misfortunes. Very likely she had taken his appearance so thoroughly for granted that it had not occurred to her to wonder how he had come to look that way. Tact could be overdone; she was less interested in him than he had thought.

'Never mind,' he said.

As they made another circuit of the floor, he caught sight of Lona at last: leaving the room. The industrialist stood by himself, seemingly baffled. Instantly Burris came to a halt. His partner looked a question at him.

'Excuse me. Perhaps she's ill.'

Not ill: just sulking. He found her in the room, face down on the bed. When he put his hand on her bare back, she shivered and rolled away from him. He could not say anything to her. They slept far apart, and when his dream of Manipool came to him, he managed to choke off his screams before they began, and sat up, rigid, until the terror passed.

Neither of them mentioned the episode in the morning.

They went sight-seeing, via power-sled. Titan's hotel-and-spaceport complex lay near the center of a smallish plateau bordered by immense mountains. Here, as on Luna, peaks that dwarfed Everest were plentiful. It seemed incongruous that such small worlds would have such great ranges, but so it was. A hundred miles or so to the west of the hotel was Martinelli Glacier, a vast creeping river of ice coiling for hundreds of miles down out of the heart of the local Himalayas. The glacier terminated, improbably enough, in the galaxy-famed Frozen Waterfall. Which every visitor to Titan was obliged to visit, and which Burris and Lona visited, too.

There were lesser sights en route that Burris found more deeply stirring. The swirling methane clouds and tufts of frozen ammonia ornamenting the naked mountains, for example, giving them the look of mountains in a Sung scroll. Or the dark lake of methane half an hour's drive from the dome. In its waxen depths dwelled the small, durable living things of Titan, creatures that were more or less mollusks and arthropods, but rather less than more. They were equipped for breathing and drinking methane. With life of any sort as scarce as it was in this solar system, Burris found it fascinating to view these rarities in their native habitat. Around the rim of the lake he saw their food: Titanweeds, ropy greasy plants, dead white in color, capable of enduring this hellish climate in perfect comfort.

The sled rolled on toward the Frozen Waterfall.

There it was: blue-white, glinting in Saturnlight, suspended over an enormous void. The beholders made the obligatory sighs and gasps. No one left the sled, for the winds were savage out there, and the breathing-suits could not be entirely trusted to protect one against the corrosive atmosphere.

They circled the waterfall, viewing the sparkling arch of ice from three sides. Then came the bad news from their cicerone: 'Storm coming up. We're heading back.'

The storm came, long before they reached the comfort of the dome. First there was rain, a sleety downpour of precipitated ammonia that rattled on the roof of their sled, and then clouds of ammonia-crystal snow, driven by the wind. The sled pushed on with difficulty. Burris had never seen snow come down so heavily or so fast. The wind churned and uprooted it, piling it into cathedrals and forests. Straining a little, the power-sled avoided new dunes and nosed around sudden barricades. Most of the passengers looked imperturbable. They exclaimed on the beauty of the storm. Burris, who knew how close they all were to entombment, sat moodily in silence. Death might bring peace at last, but if he could choose his death he did not mean to choose being buried alive. Already he could taste the acrid foulness as the air began to give out and the whining motors fed their exhaust back into the passenger compartment. Imagination, nothing more. He tried to enjoy the beauty of the storm.

Nevertheless, it was a source of great relief to enter the warmth and safety of the dome once again.

He and Lona quarreled again soon after their return. There was even less reason for this quarrel than for any of the others. But very swiftly it reached a level of real malevolence.

'You didn't look at me the whole trip, Minner!'

'I looked at the scenery. That's why we're here.'

'You could take my hand. You could smile.'

'I –'

'Am I that boring?'

He was weary of retreating. 'As a matter of fact, you are! You're a dull, dreary, ignorant little girl! All this is wasted on you! Everything! You can't appreciate food, clothing, sex, travel . . .'

'And what are you? Just a hideous freak!'

'That makes two of us.'

'Am I a freak?' she shrilled. 'It doesn't show. I'm a human being, at least. What are you?'

That was when he sprang at her.

His smooth fingers closed around her throat. She battered at him, pounded him with her fists, clawed his cheeks with raking nails. But she could not break his skin, and that roused her to smoldering fury. He gripped her firmly, shaking her, making her head roll wildly on its mooring, and all the while she kicked and punched. Through his arteries surged all the by-products of rage.

I could kill her so easily, he thought.

But the very act of pausing to let a coherent concept roll through his mind calmed him. He released her. He stared at his hands, she at him. There were mottled marks on her throat that nearly matched the blotches newly sprung out on his face. Gasping, she stepped away from him. She did not speak. Her hand, shaking, pointed at him.

Fatigue clubbed him to his knees.

All his strength vanished at once. His joints gave way, and he slipped, melting, unable even to brace himself with his hands. He lay prone, calling her name. He had never felt this weak before, not even while he had been recuperating from what had been done to him on Manipool.

This is what it's like to be bled white, he told himself. The leeches have been at me! God, will I ever be able to stand again? 'Help!' he cried soundlessly. 'Lona, where are you?'

When he was strong enough to lift his head, he discovered that she was gone. He did not know how much time had passed. Weakly he pulled himself up inch by inch and sat on the edge of the bed until the worst of the feebleness was over. Was it a judgment upon him for striking her? Each time they had quarreled he had felt this sickness come upon him.

'Lona?'

He went into the hall, staying close to the side partition. Probably he looked drunk to the well-groomed women who sailed past him. They smiled. He tried to return the smiles.

He did not find her.

Somehow, hours later, he discovered Aoudad. The little man looked apprehensive.

'Have you seen her?' Burris croaked.

'Halfway to Ganymede by now. She left on the dinner flight.'

'Left?'

Aoudad nodded. 'Nick went with her. They're going back to Earth. What did you do – slam her around some?'

'You let her go?' Burris muttered. 'You permitted her to walk out? What's Chalk going to say about that?'

'Chalk knows. Don't you think we checked with him first? He said, sure, if she wants to come home, let her come home. Put her on the next ship out. So we did. Hey, you look pale, Burris. I thought with your skin you couldn't get pale!'

'When does the next ship after hers leave?'

'Tomorrow night. You aren't going to go chasing her, are you?'

'What else?'

Grinning, Aoudad said, 'You'll never get anywhere that way. Let her go. This place is full of women who'd be glad to take her place. You'd be amazed how many. Some of them know I'm with you, and they come up to me, wanting me to fix you up with them. It's the face, Minner. The face fascinates them.'

Burris turned away from him.

141

Aoudad said, 'You're shaken up. Listen, let's go have a drink!'

Without looking back, Burris replied, 'I'm tired. I want to rest.'

'Should I send one of the women to you after a while?'

'Is that your idea of rest?'

'Well, matter of fact, yes.' He laughed pleasantly. 'I don't mind taking care of them myself, you understand, but it's you they want. You.'

'Can I call Ganymede? Maybe I can talk to her while her ship's refueling.'

Aoudad caught up with him. 'She's gone, Burris. You ought to forget her now. What did she have besides problems? Just a skinny little kid! You didn't even get along well with her. I know. I saw. All you did was shout at each other. What do you need her for? Now, let me tell you about – '

'Are you carrying any relaxers?'

'You know they won't do you any good.'

Burris held out his hand anyway. Aoudad shrugged and put a relaxer into it. Burris touched the tube to his skin. The illusion of tranquility might be worth nearly as much as the genuine article now. He thanked Aoudad and walked sharply toward his room, alone.

On the way he passed a woman whose hair was spun pink glass and whose eyes were amethysts. Her costume was chastely immodest. Her voice, feather-soft, brushed his earless cheeks. He rushed past her, trembling, and entered his room.

Twenty-seven
The Grail's True Warden

'It spoiled a lovely romance,' said Tom Nikolaides.

Lona did not smile. 'Nothing lovely about it. I was glad to get away.'

'Because he tried to choke you?'

'That was only at the very end. It was bad a long time before that. You don't have to get hurt that way in order to get hurt.'

Nikolaides peered deep into her eyes. He understood, or pretended he did. 'True enough. It's too bad, but we all knew it couldn't last.'

'Including Chalk?'

'Especially Chalk. He predicted the breakup. It's remarkable how much mail we've had on it. The whole universe seems to think it's a terrible thing that you two split.'

Lona flashed a quick, empty smile. Standing, she paced the long room in choppy strides. The plaques mounted to her heels clicked against the polished floor. 'Will Chalk be here soon?' she asked.

'Soon. He's a very busy man. But the moment he reaches the building, we'll take you to him.'

'Nick, will he really give me my babies?'

'Let's hope so.'

She caught up with him. Fiercely her hand caught his wrist. '*Hope* so? *Hope* so? He promised them to me!'

'But you walked out on Burris.'

'You said yourself Chalk was expecting it. The romance wasn't supposed to last forever. Now it's over, and I kept my part of the bargain, and Chalk's got to keep his.'

She felt muscles quivering in her thighs. These fancy shoes; hard to stand this way. But they made her look taller, older. It was important to look outwardly the way she had come to be inwardly. That trip with Burris had aged her five years in as many weeks. The constant tension . . . the bickering . . .

Above all, the terrible exhaustion after each quarrel . . .

She would look the fat man straight in the eye. If he tried to worm out of his promise, she'd make life difficult for him. No matter how powerful he was, he couldn't cheat her! She'd been nursemaid to that weird refugee from an alien planet long enough to have earned the right to her own babies. She –

That wasn't right, she admonished herself suddenly. *I mustn't make fun of him. He didn't ask for his troubles. And I volunteered to share them.*

Nikolaides stepped into the abrupt silence. 'Now that you're back on Earth, Lona, what are your plans?'

'To arrange for the children, first. Then I want to disappear from public life for good. I've had two rounds of publicity now, one when the babies were taken from me, one when I went off with Minner. That's enough.'

'Where will you go? Will you leave Earth?'

'I doubt it. I'll stay. Maybe I'll write a book.' She smiled.

143

'No, that wouldn't be so good, would it? More publicity. I'll live quietly. How about Patagonia?' She peered forward. 'Do you have any idea where *he* is now?'

'Chalk?'

'Minner,' she said.

'Still on Titan, so far as I know. Aoudad's with him.'

'They've been there three weeks, then. I suppose they're having a good time.' Her lips curved fiercely.

'I know Aoudad must be,' Nikolaides said. 'Give him plenty of available women, and he'd have a good time anywhere. But I couldn't vouch for Burris. All I know is that they haven't made any move to come home yet. Still interested in him, are you?'

'*No!*'

Nikolaides put his hands to his ears. 'All right. All right. I believe you. It's just that – '

The door at the far end of the room rippled inward. A small, ugly man with long, thin lips stepped through. Lona recognized him: he was d'Amore, one of Chalk's men. She said at once, 'Has Chalk showed up yet? I've got to talk to him!'

D'Amore's unpleasant mouth produced the broadest smile she had ever seen. 'You're really asserting yourself these days, milady! No more wispy shyness, eh? But no; Chalk's not here yet. I'm waiting for him myself.' He came farther into the room, and Lona noticed that someone behind him: white-faced, mild-eyed, totally at his ease, a man of middle years who smiled in a foolish way. D'Amore said, 'Lona, this is David Melangio. He knows a few tricks. Give him the date you were born and the year; he'll tell you what day of the week it was.'

Lona gave it.

'Wednesday,' said Melangio instantly.

'How does he do that?'

'It's his gift. Call off a string of numbers for him, as fast as you can, but clearly.'

Lona called off a dozen numbers, Melangio repeated them.

'Right?' d'Amore asked, beaming.

'I'm not sure,' she said. 'I forgot them myself.' She walked over to the idiot-savant, who regarded her without interest. Looking into his eyes, Lona realized that Melangio was another freak, all trick, no soul. She wondered, chilled, if they were hatching a new love affair for her.

Nikolaides said, 'Why'd you bring him back? I thought Chalk had let his option go.'

'Chalk thought Miss Kelvin would like to talk to him,' d'Amore replied. 'He asked me to bring Melangio over.'

'What am I supposed to say to him?' Lona asked.

'D'Amore smiled. 'How would I know?'

She drew the long-lipped man aside and whispered, 'He's not right in the head, is he?'

'I'd say he's missing something there, yes.'

'So Chalk's got another project for me? Am I supposed to hold *his* hand now?'

It was like asking the wall. D'Amore merely said, 'Take him inside, sit down, talk. Chalk probably won't be here for another hour yet.'

There was an adjoining room, with a floating glass table and several lounge chairs. She and Melangio went in, and the door closed with the finality of a cell door.

Silence. Stares.

He said, 'Ask me anything about dates. Anything.'

He rocked rhythmically back and forth. His smile did not fade at any moment. He was about seven years old mentally, Lona thought.

'Ask me when George Washington died. Ask me. Or anybody else. Anybody important.'

'Abraham Lincoln,' she sighed.

'April 15, 1865. Do you know how old he'd be if he were still alive today?' He told her, instantly, down to the day. It sounded right to her. He looked pleased with himself.

'How do you do it?'

'I don't know. I just can. I always have been able to. I can remember the weather and all the dates.' He giggled. 'Do you envy me?'

'Not very much.'

'Some people do. They wish they could learn how. Mr Chalk would like to know how. He wants you to marry me, you know.'

Lona winced. Trying not to be cruel, she said, 'Did he tell you that?'

'Oh, no. Not with words. But I know. He wants us to be together. Like you used to be, when you were with the man with the funny face. Chalk enjoyed that. Especially when you had arguments with him. I was with Mr Chalk once, and he got red in the face and chased me out of the room, and later he called me back. It must have been when you and the other one were having a fight.'

Lona groped for an understanding of all this. 'Can you read minds, David?'

'No.'

'Can Chalk?'

'No. Not *read*. It doesn't come in words. It comes in feelings. He reads feelings. I can tell. And he likes unhappy feelings. He wants us to be unhappy together, because that would make him happy.'

Perplexed, Lona leaned toward Melangio and said, 'Do you like women, David?'

'I like my mother. I sometimes like my sister. Even though they hurt me a lot when I was young.'

'Have you ever wanted to get married?'

'Oh, no! Married is for grown-ups!'

'And how old are you?'

'Forty years, eight months, three weeks, two days. I don't know how many hours. They won't tell me what time I was born.'

'You poor bastard.'

'You're sorry for me because they won't tell me what time I was born.'

'I'm sorry for you,' she said. 'Period. But I can't do anything for you, David. I've used up all my niceness. Now people have to start being nice to me.'

'I'm nice to you.'

'Yes, you are. You're very nice.' Impulsively she took his hand in hers. Her skin was smooth and cool. Not as smooth as Burris's, though, nor as cool. Melangio shivered at the contact, but allowed her to squeeze the hand. After a moment she let go and went to the wall and ran her hands over the side of the room until the door opened. She stepped through and saw Nikolaides and d'Amore murmuring to each other.

'Chalk wants to see you now,' d'Amore said. 'Did you enjoy your little visit with David?'

'He's charming. Where's Chalk?'

Chalk was in his throne-room, perched on high. Lona clambered up the crystal rungs. As she approached the fat man, she felt old timidnesses returning. She had learned how to cope with people lately, but coping with Chalk might be beyond her grasp.

He rocked in his huge chair. His broad face creased in what she took to be a smile.

'So nice to see you again. Did you enjoy your travels?'

'Very interesting. And now, my babies – '

'Please, Lona, don't rush. Have you met David?'

'Yes.'

'So pitiful. So much in need of help. What do you think of his gift?'

'We had a deal,' Lona said. 'I took care of Minner, you got me some of my babies. I don't want to talk about Melangio.'

'You broke up with Burris sooner than I had expected,' said Chalk. 'I haven't completed all the arrangements concerning your children.'

'You're going to get them for me?'

'In a short while. But not quite yet. This is a difficult negotiation, even for me. Lona, will you oblige me while you're waiting for the children? Help David, the way you helped Burris. Bring some light into his life. I'd like to see the two of you together. A warm, maternal person like you – '

'This is a trick, isn't it?' she said suddenly. 'You'll play with me forever! One zombie after another for me to cuddle! Burris, Melangio, and then who knows what next? No. No. We made a deal. I want my babies. *I want my babies.*'

Sonic dampers were whirring to cut down the impact of her shouts. Chalk looked startled. Somehow he appeared both pleased and angered at once by this show of spirit. His body seemed to puff and expand until he weighed a million pounds.

'You cheated me,' she said, quieter now. 'You never meant to give them back to me!'

She leaped. She would scrape gobbets of flesh from the fat face.

From the ceiling, instantly, descended a fine mesh of golden threads. Lona hit it, rebounded, surged forward again. She could not reach Chalk. He was shielded.

Nikolaides, d'Amore. They seized her arms. She lashed out with her weighted shoes.

'She's overwrought,' said Chalk. 'She needs calming.'

Something stung her left thigh. She sagged and was still.

Twenty-eight

Cry, What Shall I Cry?

He was growing weary of Titan. He had taken to the icy moon as to a drug after Lona's departure. But now he was numb. Nothing Aoudad could say or do . . . or get for him . . . would keep him here any longer.

Elise lay naked beside him. High overhead, the Frozen Waterfall hung in motionless cascade. They had rented their own power-sled and had come out by themselves, to park at the glacier's mouth and make love by the glimmer of Saturn-light on frozen ammonia.

'Are you sorry I came here to you, Minner?' she asked.

'Yes.' He could be blunt with her.

'Still miss her? You didn't need her.'

'I hurt her. Needlessly.'

'And what did she do to you?'

'I don't want to talk about her with you.' He sat up and put his hands on the controls of the sled. Elise sat up, too, pressing her flesh against him. In this strange light she looked whiter than ever. Did she have blood in that plump body? She was white as death. He started the sled, and it crawled slowly along the edge of the glacier, heading away from the dome. Pools of methane lay here and there. Burris said, 'Would you object if I opened the roof of the sled, Elise?'

'We'd die.' She didn't sound worried.

'You'd die. I'm not sure I would. How do I know this body can't breathe methane?'

'It isn't likely.' She stretched, voluptuously, languidly. 'Where are you going?'

'Sight-seeing.'

'It might not be safe here. You might break through the ice.'

'Then we'd die. It would be restful, Elise.'

The sled hit a crunching tongue of new ice. It bounced slightly, and so did Elise. Idly Burris watched the quiver ripple its way all through her abundant flesh. She had been with him a week now. Aoudad had produced her. There was much to

148

be said for her voluptuousness, little for her soul. Burris wondered if poor Prolisse had known what sort of wife he had taken.

She touched his skin. She was always touching him, as if reveling in the wrongness of his texture. 'Love me again,' she said.

'Not now. Elise, what do you desire in me?'

'All of you.'

'There's a universe full of men who can keep you happy in bed. What in particular do I have for you?'

'The Manipool changes.'

'You love me for the way I look?'

'I love you because you're unusual.'

'What about blind men? One-eyed men? Hunchbacks? Men with no noses?'

'There aren't any. Everyone gets a prosthetic now. Everyone's perfect.'

'Except me.'

'Yes. Except you.' Her nails dug into his skin. 'I can't scratch you. I can't make you sweat. I can't even look at you without feeling a little queasy. *That's* what I desire in you.'

'Queasiness?'

'You're being silly.'

'You're a masochist, Elise. You want to grovel. You pick the weirdest thing in the system and throw yourself at him and call it love, but it isn't love, it isn't even sex, it's just self-torture. Right?'

She looked at him queerly.

'You like to be hurt,' he said. He put his hand over one of her breasts, spreading the fingers wide to encompass all the soft, warm bulk of it. Then he closed his hand. Elise winced. Her delicate nostrils flared and her eyes began to tear. But she said nothing as he squeezed. Her respiration grew more intense; it seemed to him that he could feel the thunder of her heart. She would absorb any quantity of this pain without a whimper, even if he tore the white globe of flesh from her body entirely. When he released her, there were six white imprints against the whiteness of her flesh. In a moment they began to turn red. She looked like a tigress about to spring. Above them, the Frozen Waterfall rushed downward in eternal stillness. Would it begin to flow? Would Saturn drop from the heavens and brush Titan with his whirling rings?

'I'm leaving for Earth tomorrow,' he told her.

She lay back. Her body was receptive. 'Make love to me, Minner.'

'I'm going back alone. To look for Lona.'

'You don't need her. Stop trying to annoy me.' She tugged at him. 'Lie down beside me. I want to look at Saturn again while you have me.'

He ran his hand along the silkiness of her. Her eyes glittered. He whispered, 'Let's get out of the sled. Let's run naked to that lake and swim in it.'

Methane clouds puffed about them. The temperature outside would make Antarctica in winter seem tropical. Would they die first from freezing, or from the poison in their lungs? They'd never reach the lake. He saw them sprawled on the snowy dune, white on white, rigid as marble. He'd last longer than she would, holding his breath as she toppled and fell, as she flopped about, flesh caressed by the hydrocarbon bath. But he wouldn't last long.

'Yes!' she cried. 'We'll swim! And afterwards we'll make love beside the lake!'

She reached for the control that would lift the transparent roof of the sled. Burris admired the tension and play of her muscles as her arm stretched toward it, as her hand extended itself, as ligaments and tendons functioned beautifully under the smooth skin from wrist to ankle. One leg was folded up underneath her, the other nicely thrust forward to echo the line of her arm. Her breasts were drawn upward; her throat, which had a tendency toward loose flesh, was now taut. Altogether she was a handsome sight. She needed only to twist a lever and the roof would spring back, exposing them to the virulent atmosphere of Titan. Her slender fingers were on the lever. Burris ceased to contemplate her. He clamped his hand on her arm even as her muscles were tensing, pulled her away, hurled her back on the couch. She landed in a wanton way. As she sat up, he slapped her across the lips. Blood trickled to her chin and her eyes sparkled in pleasure. He hit her again, chopping blows that made the flesh of her leap about. She panted. She clutched at him. The odor of lust assailed his nostrils.

He hit her one more time. Then, realizing he was giving her only what she wanted, he moved away from her and tossed her her discarded breathing-suit.

'Put it on. We're going back to the dome.'

She was the incarnation of raw hunger. She writhed in what

150

could have been self-parody of desire. She called hoarsely to him.

'We're going back,' he said. 'And we aren't going back naked.'

Reluctantly she dressed herself.

She would have opened the roof, he told himself. She would have gone swimming with me in the methane lake.

He started the sled and sped back to the hotel.

'Are you really leaving for Earth tomorrow?'

'Yes. I've booked passage.'

'Without me?'

'Without you.'

'What if I followed you again?'

'I can't stop you. But it won't do you any good.'

The sled came to the airlock of the dome. He drove in and returned the sled at the rental desk. Elise looked rumpled and sweaty within her breathing-suit.

Burris, going to his room, closed the door quickly and locked it. Elise knocked a few times. He made no reply, and she went away. He rested his head in his hands. The fatigue was coming back, the utter weariness that he had not felt since the final quarrel with Lona. But it passed after a few minutes.

An hour later the hotel management came for him. Three men, grim-faced, saying very little. Burris donned the breathing-suit they gave him and went out into the open with them.

'She's under the blanket. We'd like you to identify her before we bring her in.'

Subtle crystals of ammonia snow had fallen on the blanket. They blew aside as Burris peeled it back. Elise, naked, seemed to be hugging the ice. The spots on her breast where his fingertips had dug in had turned deep purple. He touched her. Like marble she was.

'She died instantly,' said a voice at his elbow.

Burris looked up. 'She had a great deal to drink this afternoon. Perhaps that explains it.'

He stayed in his room the rest of that evening and through the morning that followed. At midday he was summoned for the ride to the spaceport, and within four hours he was aloft, bound for Earth via Ganymede. He said little to anyone all the while.

Twenty-nine

Dona Nobis Pacem

She had come, washed up by the tides, to the Martlet Towers. There she lived in a single room, rarely going out, changing her clothes infrequently, speaking to no one. She knew the truth now, and the truth had imprisoned her.

. . . and then he found her.

She stood bird-like, ready for flight. 'Who's there?'

'Minner.'

'What do you want?'

'Let me in, Lona. Please.'

'How did you find me here?'

'Some guesswork. Some bribery. Open the door, Lona.'

She opened it for him. He looked unchanged over the weeks since she had last seen him. He stepped through, not smiling his equivalent of a smile, not touching her, not kissing. The room was almost in darkness. She moved to light it, but he cut her off with a brusque gesture.

'I'm sorry it's so shabby,' she said.

'It looks fine. It looks just like the room I lived in. But that was two buildings over.'

'When did you get back to Earth, Minner?'

'Several weeks ago. I've been searching hard.'

'Have you seen Chalk?'

Burris nodded. 'I didn't get much from him.'

'Neither did I.' Lona turned to the food conduit. 'Something to drink?'

'Thanks, no.'

He sat down. There was something blessedly familiar about the elaborate way he coiled himself into her chair, moving all his extra joints so carefully. Just the sight of it made her pulse-rate climb.

He said, 'Elise is dead. She killed herself on Titan.'

Lona made no response.

He said, 'I didn't ask her to come to me. She was a very confused person. Now she's at rest.'

'She's better at suicide than I am,' Lona said.

'You haven't –'

'No. Not again. I've been living quietly, Minner. Should I admit the truth? I've been waiting for you to come to me.'

'All you had to do was let somebody know where you were!'

'It was more complicated than that. I couldn't advertise myself. But I'm glad you're here. I have so much to tell you!'

'Such as?'

'Chalk isn't going to have any of my children transferred to me. I've been checking. He couldn't do it if he wanted to, and he doesn't want to. It was just a convenient lie to get me to work for him.'

Burris's eyes flickered. 'You mean, to get you to keep company with me?'

'That's it. I won't hide anything now, Minner. You already know, more or less. There had to be a price before I'd go with you. Getting the children was the price. I kept my end of the bargain, but Chalk isn't keeping his.'

'I knew that you'd been bought, Lona. I was bought, too. Chalk found my price to come out of hiding and conduct an interplanetary romance with a certain girl.'

'Transplant into a new body?'

'Yes,' Burris said.

'You aren't going to get that, any more than I'm going to get my babies,' she said flatly. 'Am I killing any of your illusions? Chalk cheated you the way he cheated me.'

'I've been discovering that,' Burris said, 'since my return. The body-transfer project is at least twenty years away. Not five years. They may never solve some of the problems. They can switch a brain into a new body and keep it alive, but the – what shall I say – *soul* goes. They get a zombie. Chalk knew all that when he offered me his deal.'

'He got his romance out of us. And we got nothing out of him.' Rising, Lona walked around the room. She came to the tiny potted cactus that she had once given to Burris and rubbed the tip of one finger idly over its bristly surface. Burris seemed to notice the cactus for the first time. He looked pleased.

Lona said, 'Do you know why he brought us together, Minner?'

'To make money on the publicity. He picks two used-up people and tricks them into coming part way back to life, and tells the world about it, and –'

153

'No. Chalk has enough money. He didn't give a damn about the profit.'

'Then what?' he asked.

'An idiot told me the real thing. An idiot named Melangio, who does a trick with calendars. Perhaps you've seen him on vid. Chalk used him in some shows.'

'No.'

'I met him at Chalk's place. Sometimes a fool speaks truth. He said Chalk's a drinker of emotion. He lives on fear, pain, envy, grief. Chalk sets up situations that he can exploit. Bring two people together who are so battered that they can't possibly allow happiness to take hold of them, and watch them suffer. And feed. And drain them.'

Burris looked startled. 'Even at long range? He could feed even when we were at Luna Tivoli? Or on Titan?'

'Each time we quarreled . . . we felt so tired afterward. As if we'd lost blood. As if we were hundreds of years old.'

'Yes!'

'That was Chalk,' she said. 'Getting fatter on our suffering. He knew we'd hate each other, and that was what he wanted. Can there be a vampire of emotion?'

'So all the promises were false,' he whispered. 'We were puppets. If it's true.'

'I know it's true.'

'Because an idiot told you so?'

'A very wise idiot, Minner. Besides, work it all out for yourself. Think of everything Chalk ever said to you. Think of all that happened. Why was Elise always waiting in the wings to throw her arms around you? Don't you think it was deliberate, part of a campaign to infuriate me? We were tied together by our strangeness . . . by our hatred. And Chalk loved it.'

Burris stared at her quietly a long moment. Then, without a word, he went to the door, opened it, stepped out into the hall, and pounced on something. Lona could not see what he was doing until he returned with a struggling, squirming Aoudad.

'I thought you'd be out there somewhere,' Burris said. 'Come in. Come in. We'd like to talk with you.'

'Minner, don't hurt him,' Lona said. 'He's only a tool.'

'He can answer some questions. Won't you, Bart?'

Aoudad moistened his lips. His eyes flicked warily from face to face.

Burris hit him.

The hand came up with blinding speed. Lona didn't see it, and neither did Aoudad, but the man's head shot back and he thumped heavily into the wall. Burris gave him no chance to defend himself. Aoudad clung blearily to the wall as the blows landed. Finally he sagged, eyes still open, face bloody.

'Talk to us,' Burris said. 'Talk to us about Duncan Chalk.'

Later they left her room. Aoudad remained behind, sleeping peacefully. In the street below they found his car, waiting on an uptake ramp. Burris started it and headed it toward Chalk's office building.

'We were making a mistake,' he said, 'trying to change ourselves back to what we were. We are our own essences. I am the mutilated starman. You are the girl with a hundred babies. It's a mistake to try to flee.'

'Even if we could flee.'

'Even if we could. They could give me a different body someday, yes, and where would that put me? I'd have lost what I am now, and I'd have gained nothing. I'd lose myself. And they could give you two of your babies, perhaps, but what about the other ninety-eight? What's done is done. The fact of your essence has absorbed you. And mine me. Is that too cloudy for you?'

'You're saying that we have to face up squarely to what we are, Minner.'

'That's it. That's it. No more running away. No more brooding. No more hatred.'

'But the world – the normal people – '

'It's us against them. They want to devour us. They want to put us in the freak show. We have to fight back, Lona!'

The car halted. There was the low, windowless building. They entered, and, yes, Chalk would see them, if they would only wait awhile in an outer room. They waited. They sat side by side, scarcely looking at each other. In her hands Lona held the potted cactus. It was the only possession she had taken from her room. They were welcome to the rest.

Burris said quietly, 'Turn the anguish outward. There's no other way we can fight.'

Leontes d'Amore appeared. 'Chalk will see you now,' he said.

Up the crystal rungs. Toward the immense figure in the high throne.

155

'Lona? Burris? Together again?' Chalk asked. He laughed boomingly and tapped his belly. He clapped his hands on the columns of his thighs.

'You dined well on us, didn't you, Chalk?' Burris asked.

The laughter died away. Abruptly Chalk was sitting up, tense, wary. He seemed almost to be a thin man now, ready to take to his heels.

Lona said, 'It's nearly evening. We've brought you your dinner, Duncan.'

They stood facing him, Burris slipped his arm around her slender waist. Chalk's lips moved. No sounds came out, and his hand did not quite reach the alarm lever on his desk. The pudgy fingers fanned wide. Chalk contemplated them.

'For you,' Burris said. 'With our compliments. Our love.'

Shared emotion flooded from them in shining waves.

It was a torrent Chalk could not withstand. He moved from side to side, buffeted by the furious stream, one side of his mouth quirking upward, then the other. A trail of spittle appeared on his chin. His head jerked sharply three times. Robot-like, he crossed and uncrossed his thick arms.

Burris clung so tightly to Lona that her ribs protested.

Did flames dance crackling along Chalk's desk? Did rivers of raw electrons become visible and glow green before him? He writhed, unable to move, as they gave him their souls in passionate intensity. He fed. But he could not digest. He grew more bloated. His face was bright with sweat.

No word was spoken.

Sink, white whale! Lash your mighty flukes and go down!

Retro me, Satanas!

Here's fire; come, Faustus, set it on.

Glad tidings from great Lucifer.

Chalk moved now. He spun in his chair, breaking from stasis, slamming his fleshy arms again and again onto the desk. He was bathed in the blood of the Albatross. He quivered, jerked, quivered again. The scream that left his lips was no more than a thin, feeble whine delivered by a gaping maw. Now he was strung taut, now he twanged with the rhythms of destruction . . .

And then came slackness.

The eyeballs rolled. The lips drooped. The massive shoulders slumped. The cheeks sagged.

Consummatum est; this bill is ended.

All three figures were motionless: those who had hurled

their souls, and he who had received them. One of the three would never move again.

Burris was the first to recover. It was an effort even to draw breath. To give power to his lips and tongue was a colossal task. He swung around, recovering the knowledge of his limbs, and put his hands on Lona. She was death-pale, frozen in her place. As he touched her, the strength seemed to flow swiftly back into her.

'We can't stay here any longer,' he said gently.

They left, slowly, dwelling now in extreme old age, but growing younger as they descended the crystal rungs. Vitality returned. It would be many days before they had fully replenished themselves, but at least there would be no further drain.

No one interfered with them as they left the building.

Night had fallen. Winter was past, and the gray haze of a spring evening covered the city. The stars were barely visible. A faint chill still lingered, but neither of them shivered in the coolness.

'This world has no place for us,' Burris said.

'It would only try to eat us. As he tried.'

'We defeated him. But we can't defeat a whole world.'

'Where will we go?'

Burris looked upward. 'Come with me to Manipool. We'll visit the demons for Sunday tea.'

'Are you serious?'

'Yes. Will you go there with me?'

'Yes.'

They walked toward the car.

'How do you feel?' he asked.

'Very tired. So tired I can scarcely move. But I feel alive. More alive with every step. For the first time, Minner, I feel really alive.'

'As do I.'

'Your body – does it hurt you now?'

'I love my body,' he said.

'Despite the pain?'

'Because of the pain,' he said. 'It shows that I live. That I feel.' He turned to her and took the cactus from her hands. The clouds parted. The thorns gleamed by starlight. 'To be alive – to feel, even to feel pain – how important that is, Lona.'

He broke a small limb from the plant and pressed it into

157

the flesh of her hand. The thorns sank deep. She flinched only for a moment. Tiny droplets of blood appeared. From the cactus she took a second limb, and pressed it to him. It was difficult, breaking through that impervious skin of his, but the thorns did penetrate at last. He smiled as the blood began to flow. He touched her wounded hand to his lips, and she his hand to hers.

'We bleed,' she said. 'We feel. We live.'

'Pain is instructive,' said Burris, and they walked more quickly.

NEL BESTSELLERS

War

T027 066	COLDITZ: THE GERMAN STORY	Reinhold Eggers	50p
T020 827	COLDITZ RECAPTURED	Reinhold Eggers	50p
T020 584	THE GOOD SHEPHERD	C. S. Forester	40p
T012 999	PQ 17 – CONVOY TO HELL	Lund & Ludlam	30p
T026 299	TRAWLERS GO TO WAR	Lund & Ludlam	50p
T025 438	LILLIPUT FLEET	A. Cecil Hampshire	50p
T018 032	ARK ROYAL	Kenneth Poolman	40p
T027 198	THE GREEN BERET	Hilary St George Saunders	50p
T027 171	THE RED BERET	Hilary St George Saunders	50p

Western

T017 893	EDGE 12: THE BIGGEST BOUNTY	George Gilman	30p
T023 931	EDGE 13: A TOWN CALLED HATE	George Gilman	35p
T020 002	EDGE 14: THE BIG GOLD	George Gilman	30p
T020 754	EDGE 15: BLOOD RUN	George Gilman	35p
T022 706	EDGE 16: THE FINAL SHOT	George Gilman	35p
T024 881	EDGE 17: VENGEANCE VALLEY	George Gilman	40p
T026 604	EDGE 18: TEN TOMBSTONES TO TEXAS	George Gilman	40p
T028 135	EDGE 19: ASHES AND DUST	George Gilman	40p
T029 042	EDGE 20: SULLIVAN'S LAW	George Gilman	45p

General

T017 400	CHOPPER	Peter Cave	30p
T022 838	MAMA	Peter Cave	35p
T021 009	SEX MANNERS FOR MEN	Robert Chartham	35p
T023 206	THE BOOK OF LOVE	Dr David Delvin	90p
T028 623	CAREFREE LOVE	Dr David Delvin	60p

Mad

S006 739	MADVERTISING		70p
N766 275	MORE SNAPPY ANSWERS TO STUPID QUESTIONS		70p
N769 452	VOODOO MAD		70p
S006 741	MAD POWER		70p
S006 291	HOPPING MAD		70p

NEL P.O. BOX 11, FALMOUTH TR10 9EN, CORNWALL:

For U.K.: Customers should include to cover postage, 19p for the first book plus 9p per copy for each additional book ordered up to a maximum charge of 73p.

For B.F.P.O. and Eire: Customers should include to cover postage, 19p for the first book plus 9p per copy for the next 6 and thereafter 3p per book.

For Overseas: Customers should include to cover postage, 20p for the first book plus 10p per copy for each additional book.

Name ....

Address...

....

....

Title ....
(NOVEMBER)

Whilst every effort is made to maintain prices, new editions or printings may carry an increased price and the actual price of the edition supplied will apply.